SURVIVAL
OF THE FIERCEST

SURVIVAL OF THE FIERCEST

A SLOANE SISTERS NOVEL

BY ANNA CAREY

HARPER TEEN

An Imprint of HarperCollinsPublishers

alloyentertainment
Produced by Alloy Entertainment
151 West 26th Street, New York, NY 10001

Library of Congress catalog card number: 2009928953

ISBN 978-0-06-117578-7

Design by Andrea C. Uva

09 10 11 12 13 CG/RRDH 10 9 8 7 6 5 4 3 2 1

❖

First Edition

For Joelle

SURVIVAL

OF
THE
FIERCEST

PROLOGUE

When we last left Cate, Stella, Andie, and Lola, all was peace-ful on the Upper East Side. Winston Sloane and Emma Childs were married, and their daughters were enjoying their first moments of familial bliss.

Now their parents are leaving for their honeymoon and the girls are on their own. With a whole town house to themselves, can they play nice? Doubtful. Maybe they're a happy family now. But nothing lasts forever . . . especially not with these sisters.

WHILE THE PARENTS ARE AWAY . . . THE CHILDREN WILL PLAY

Cate Sloane stood by the foyer window, watching as a limo pulled in front of the town house. She clasped her hands together, resisting the urge to shove her father, Winston, and his new bride, Emma, out the door. They were leaving for their last-minute honeymoon to Tahiti—to go with their last-minute wedding yesterday. Which meant that for one whole week Cate had no one to answer to but Margot, a hearing-impaired retiree in leather pants. Margot was Stella and Lola's grandmother, and her new stepsisters looked as horrified by her sartorial choices as Cate.

"So we're off," Winston said. He glanced around the foyer. Stella's tall, gawky younger sister, Lola, clutched her cat, Heath Bar, in her arms. At four foot eleven, Cate's younger sister, Andie, looked like a dwarf standing beside her.

"Now, remember," Emma added as she hugged her daughters. "Grandmum will—"

"Emma, please," Margot huffed. She winked at the girls as she tousled her stiff blond hair. "Call me Margot." Her Derek Lam halter revealed her collarbone, the skin spotted like a snakeskin clutch.

"Right, listen to *Margot*." Winston shot Cate a look that said, *That means you*.

Cate grabbed Stella's arm so hard her knuckles turned white. "Forget Margot," she whispered. "*We're* in charge." Cate pictured herself and Stella lying out in their Shoshanna bikinis on the roof deck, drinking sparkling lemonade. They'd spend afternoons shopping for a fall wardrobe at Bergdorf Goodman and late evenings trying out the ginger garlic shrimp at El Quinto Pino or the carpaccio at Buzina Pop. But most importantly, an empty town house would give them the perfect opportunity to launch their new sorority: Chi Sigma.

"We should have a sleepover on the roof deck tonight," Stella said in her lilting British accent.

"I like the way you think." Cate leaned in close. "We need to plan a meet-and-greet in the garden—something to officially announce the split with Blythe."

Cate's stomach tightened just saying Blythe Finley's name. Last week, after a huge fight at the Pierre Hotel, Cate and Stella had been banished from Chi Beta Phi, the sorority Cate had founded with her best friends Blythe, Priya, and Sophie. The Chi Beta Phis had been the most popular girls at Ashton Prep since forever. And Cate had been in charge, with Blythe as her trusty second-in-command. But on Saturday, while Stella and Cate were fighting over who should be the sorority's president, Blythe staged a coup and turned Priya and Sophie against Cate. So now instead of planning her campaign for class president or her fifteenth birthday party at Butter, Cate was starting over. But she was still determined to make ninth grade her year. She couldn't let some minor detail—like losing all your "friends"—ruin it.

Margot wrapped an arm around Lola's shoulder and pointed at Winston and Emma. "You two go now! Have fun in Tahiti! We'll survive without you."

But Winston hovered in the doorway, his gaze settling on Cate and Stella. He scratched the back of his neck. "We'll call you as soon as we get there. And if you need anything at all, you have our number at the hotel."

"You said that." Cate inched forward, moving him closer to the door. "Three times."

"Right." Winston enveloped Cate in a hug. He smoothed down her dark brown hair. "Just be good."

Cate glanced sideways at Stella and smiled. "We're going to be just fine."

Emma and Winston said their final goodbyes, Emma making sure to kiss everyone on both cheeks, Euro style. Then they headed out the door.

Cate watched her dad slide into the backseat of the limo, relieved. Winston and Emma had let them stay home from school today to recover from the wedding, but tomorrow Cate would have to face Blythe, Priya, and Sophie. Blythe was probably in her bedroom right now with *Cate's* friends, planning their first Cate-free sleepover or their Saturday shopping route through SoHo. She and Stella needed to get organized—immediately.

Lola waved as the limo pulled away. "Have a brilliant time!"

she shouted. Then she trailed up the stairs, Andie following behind her.

"Well, I don't know about you, but I'm going to dig into some of that leftover wedding cake," Margot cooed. She retreated to the kitchen, while Cate and Stella stayed on the front step.

As the car rounded the corner Cate let out a deep breath. "Chi Sigma's reign has officially begun!" she cried, throwing her arms around her new stepsister. "We need to figure out where we're going to sit at lunch tomorrow, and how we're going to announce the sorority."

"Agreed." Stella nodded. "I think we should have the meet-and-greet this weekend, for a select group of ninth-grade girls. Maybe in the garden."

Cate smiled, imagining Betsy Carmichael covering the event for *Ashton News*. She'd walk around the garden, asking girls what they thought of the new sorority. *Much better than Chi Beta Phi*, Paige Mortimer would say, sipping her mojito mocktail. *Cate Sloane should have gone on her own a long time ago.*

"And maybe we could have a few of the seniors over one night," Cate added. "I've always wondered where Ally Pierce gets her vintage jewelry." Ally was the most popular senior at Ashton Prep.

Just then, Margot's voice echoed from inside the foyer. "Stella! Where are the forks? I can't find anything in this house!"

Stella put her finger in the air. "Hold that thought," she told Cate. "I'll be right back." Her blond curls bounced up and down as she strode into the foyer.

Cate stayed on the front step, enjoying the warm early

September air. She glanced down the tree-lined street. A white truck was parked in front of the town house next door, ALL-STAR MOVERS! scrawled across its side in annoyingly enthusiastic red lettering. When the Warburtons moved out last month, Cate had half-jokingly asked her dad to buy the house for her for her birthday.

Two stocky men pulled boxes out of the back of the truck, so drenched with sweat they looked like they were in a wet-T-shirt contest. The front door swung open and someone bounded down the stoop. Not just any someone: the most adorable boy Cate had ever seen.

He was tall, with thick black hair and dark, almond-shaped eyes. He wore a tight gray Haverford T-shirt and had an iPod bud in each ear. Cate sucked in a breath. He didn't belong in the Warburtons' old town house. He belonged shirtless, in a field—like in some Abercrombie & Fitch ad.

Cate twisted her dark brown hair in a ponytail as the boy ran past. "Hi," he said with a smile, nodding at Cate. She held her breath as she watched him run up Fifth Avenue.

"Hi," she whispered, five seconds too late. She tugged on the waist of her Juicy sweatpants, determined. From now on, she wasn't going anywhere—to the park, across the street, or even to the front window—without putting on her pearl earrings and her NARS cream blush.

In addition to lunches at Aureole and schmoozing with Ashton upperclassmen, Cate Sloane had a new priority on her to-do list this year: make her hot new neighbor her hot new boy-friend.

TO: Danny Plimpton
FROM: Cate Sloane
DATE: Monday, 7:13 p.m.
SUBJECT: Intel?

Dear Danny,
We've never formally met, but Betsy Carmichael mentioned you collected intel on her Haverford crush this summer. I'd like to hire you on a freelance basis. I'm interested, specifically, in my new next-door neighbor. Perhaps we could discuss more over the phone? I'm at 917-555-2032. Confidentiality is, of course, key.

Regards,
Cate Sloane

TO: Cate Sloane
FROM: Danny Plimpton
DATE: Tuesday, 9:09 a.m.
SUBJECT: The Eagle

Cate Sloane,

Thank you for requesting my services for the collection of intelligence on Eli Alexander Punch, from here on out referred to as "the Eagle." This e-mail will serve as the formal agreement: In return for services rendered, you will help me win the heart of your new stepsister, Lola Childs, from here on out referred to as "Beautiful Stranger." I saw her walking to school last week and I have not been the same since. Any information you can gather—secret likes or dislikes she has, photos, her schedule—will serve as adequate compensation. Most important, I'd like to know if she has a date yet to the Haverford Middle School formal.

I'll text you later today with more information.

Sincerely,
Danny Plimpton

Please note: This e-mail has been vetted by Kirk Plimpton, a partner from the law firm Crowley, Plimpton & Ellis.

TWO'S COMPANY, THREE'S A CLIQUE

"Let's see those necks, girls—like a swan!" Mrs. Rodriguez called from her mat as she raised her legs a perfect forty-five degrees. "Not a turtle—a swan!"

Stella was standing in the doorway of Ashton Prep's exercise room, where the fourth-period class was finishing up Pilates. Cate hovered behind her, texting on her iPhone like the apocalypse was coming. The class winced as they held their legs in the air. Stella was sweating just watching them.

"This seventh-grader at Haverford is collecting intel," Cate whispered, tucking her iPhone back into her black cropped Nike pants. "Eli is from Westport, Connecticut, he's half Japanese and half Irish, and completely single."

"Right, the mysterious Eli Punch," Stella said. Cate had been talking about their neighbor nonstop for the last twenty-four hours. So far Stella had learned he was five foot eleven, that he wore Saucony running sneakers, and that he'd be Cate's boyfriend in less than a month. But this morning, when they'd walked by the Warburtons' old town house, the windows were bare, no lights were on, and it still looked just as empty as it had five days ago. Unless Cate was a ghost whisperer, she was out of luck.

"He exists—I *saw* him." Cate squeezed the mat to her chest, like she was enveloping Eli in a hug. "He has thick black hair and perfect skin, and when he says hi, he kind of tips his chin forward like he's pointing at you with his nose." Cate made the same gesture, nodding slightly at Stella.

A stream of girls pushed out of the room, patting their foreheads with paper towels. Even with the air-conditioning blasting on high, the place still smelled of old gym clothes. Stella caught Mrs. Rodriguez admiring her own triceps, like she was in some bad Pilates infomercial.

As Cate plopped down on her mat, Paige Mortimer and Betsy Carmichael strolled past. "Hi, Cate," Paige called. She glanced around Stella, as though Priya, Sophie, and Blythe might've been hiding behind her back. "Where is everybody?" she asked.

"This *is* everybody," Cate said. "You know my stepsister Stella, right?" Paige offered Stella a weak smile. The two girls unrolled their mats near the mirror, and Betsy whispered something in Paige's ear.

Cate pulled her legs into a butterfly stretch, bouncing her knees up and down nervously. She'd only missed one day of school, but Blythe had used it to her advantage. She had already told people about the fight at the Pierre and how *she* was president of the sorority now. She even renamed them the Beta Sigma Phis. In the bathroom this morning, Cate had overheard Shelley DeWitt speculating whether or not Blythe would join Ashton's improv team, or if Blythe's new sorority was going to the Turtle Pond after school. She'd only mentioned Cate once—to say how sad it was that she was stuck hanging out with "that British girl" until Blythe forgave her. Cate could handle not being friends with Blythe. But she couldn't handle being treated like any of the hundred and two ninth-graders at Ashton. Because she wasn't just anyone. She was *Cate Sloane*. "We have to go to Jackson Hole after school, or lie out on the Great Lawn. We need people to recognize that we're a sorority." She studied Stella's face, chewing the MAC gloss off her bottom lip. "It's just hard . . . because you're still new."

Stella let those words sink in. *You're still new.* Cate might as well have said, *You have boils all over your body,* or *You have a third arm growing out of your forehead*. But Stella couldn't deny it—she'd only been at Ashton Prep for a little over a week. Even if she and Cate were friends again, the school was still as foreign as Cairo or Hong Kong. Besides Cate and the estranged Chi Beta Phis, she didn't know one single person in the upper school. Just today she'd mistaken the janitor's closet for the loo. "Let's have the meet-and-greet tomorrow then," Stella offered. "The sooner the better."

She glanced at the clock on the wall. Right now it was four twelve in London, which meant her best friends Pippa and Bridget were done at Millshire Prep for the day. She'd talked to Pippa once since she'd been in New York. For less than three minutes, online. Of course it would be hard to keep in touch with the time difference, Stella had always known that. But they had her new mobile number, the number at the ouse, and her new address. Every day she checked the mailbox—looking for a card, a care package, anything—but all she found was Winston's *Financial Times* and some flyers for Venezia Pizza.

Just then, Blythe strolled into the room, Sophie and Priya trailing behind her. They were all wearing identical gym clothes: gray yoga pants and purple V-neck tank tops.

"Funny seeing you here," Blythe called as she unrolled her mat in the far corner. She'd spent two full days sending threatening texts, assuming Cate and Stella would beg and bribe for her forgiveness (FYI: DECIDING ON UR 1ST TRIAL. THERE'S A PURPLE BOTKIER BAG I WANT AT NORDSTROM, HAVING A BETA SIGMA PHI PARTY 2NIGHT—2 BAD U GUYS CAN'T COME . . .) but Cate had insisted they ignore Blythe, and Stella agreed. They didn't want to announce Chi Sigma until the meet-and-greet in the garden. Stella stretched over her toes, pretending to have a sudden interest in her shins.

"Pathetic!" Cate hissed, as she eyed their V-neck tanks. "I never made the Chi Beta Phis wear matching outfits—the most important part of fashion is *individuality*. I bet you from now on they only wear shirts that show off Blythe's boobs." A few more girls trickled in as Blythe and the Beta Sigma Phis sat down on their mats. Cate reached toward her ankle, but her gaze was still on her old friends.

"Forget them," Stella whispered, knowing it was easier said than done. She'd just met the girls, but even she was having trouble forgetting them . . . and everything else that had happened last week. She and Cate still hadn't talked about their fight, and Cate certainly hadn't apologized. Not for telling her friends about her father's affair with the pop singer Cloud McClean, not for putting Stella "in trials" to make her prove she was worthy enough to be a member of Chi Beta Phi. Even at the wedding, as they danced to the band's rendition of "Rock Your Body," Cate kept glancing at the door. Stella couldn't help but wonder if she was waiting for her *real* friends to arrive.

Cate gripped her shin with her sweaty palm, trying hard not to look up. The last time she'd spoken to her friends was at the Pierre. She'd managed to go three whole days without responding to Blythe's texts or talking to Sophie and Priya on IM. But she could barely eat, and when she heard Blythe's name her entire body tensed up. Everything—the framed photos on her dresser, the four matching sleeping bags in her closet, or the Feist songs Priya had put on her iPod—reminded her of her ex-friends.

She felt for the Tiffany locket on her neck. Blythe had given it to her as a gift so her mom could be with her, always, wherever she went. Cate knew Blythe, Priya, and Sophie were mad, but her father had gotten married two days ago, and none of them had even asked her about it. Priya said nothing in homeroom, and Sophie barely looked at her when she passed her in the hall. It was as though their Beta Sigma Phi hazing involved Cate Sloane lobotomies.

Cate glanced across the room just as Blythe approached. She was swinging a disinfectant spray bottle in her hand, Priya and Sophie close behind her. Sophie offered a quick little wave, looking like she was on the verge of tears. She was never good at fighting with anyone. Even when Priya slow danced with

Haverford crush at the eighth-grade bon voyage dance, ₃ₙₑ d only stayed mad for twenty minutes.

"Oh, how the mighty have fallen," Blythe cooed, her gaze settling on Cate. She put her hands on her hips, sticking out her newest assets.

"Wow." Cate glanced at Blythe's yoga pants. "I'm surprised you managed to put a whole outfit together by yourself. It must be hard for you to function without my running commentary on your life." As the former president, Cate was always the one who gave final verdicts on outfits, the one who marked everyone's birthdays (and half birthdays) on her iCalendar, and planned every sleepover three weeks in advance so they never conflicted with Blythe's weekends in L.A. with her dad, or the times when Priya's sister was home.

"I'm doing just fine—thanks for your concern." Blythe turned to Stella. "Ready for your first trial? My dad's visiting next weekend with my baby brother—I could use someone on twenty-four-hour diaper duty."

"Isn't that what Priya and Sophie are for?" Stella asked innocently.

Priya's nose scrunched in disgust. "Very funny," she mumbled.

"I don't want to change diapers," Sophie whispered nervously, tugging on a flattened strand of light brown hair.

Blythe ignored her. She cracked her knuckles so loud the entire room turned around. Eleanor Donner and her friends were perched on the edge of their mats, as though they were watching an episode of *The Real World: Ashton Prep*. "I need to see some more enthusiasm, girls. It's going to be an incredibly busy year for me, being the new *president* of Beta Sigma Phi and all." She paused, as though she were appreciating the sound of the word *president*. "I don't have time for your games."

Cate could feel Paige and Betsy's eyes on them, watching from the other side of the room. "We're not playing games," she said through clenched teeth.

Blythe pressed the disinfectant bottle into Cate's hands. "You can start by wiping down my mat. Kimberly Berth was practicing over there, and now it reeks of her Britney Spears perfume."

"Actually," Cate said coolly, "there won't be any trials. We're starting our own sorority." She pressed the spray bottle back into Blythe's hand, the pink liquid sloshing around inside. Cate watched Blythe's smile fall.

"So, in other words," Stella hissed, "wipe down your own bloody mat." She was good at a lot of things—still-life drawing, talking Bridget and Pippa out of boy-induced moping, finding Heath Bar whenever Lola frantically claimed he'd "run away"— but she'd never been good at taking orders. "We have more important things to worry about. It's very demanding, being in the most popular clique at Ashton Prep."

Blythe leaned down, like she was addressing two small dogs. "Nice try, but two people isn't a clique," she pointed out. "It's just *friends*." She smiled triumphantly. The Beta Sigma Phis stalked back to the other side of the room and spread out on their mats, a bundle of gray legs and purple torsos.

"What does Blythe know?" Stella whispered under her breath. She reached her arms above her head.

Cate glanced around. There, in front of the room, Eleanor

and her four friends were stretching against the wall. There, by the mirror, Shelley DeWitt was practicing plank with Betsy Carmichael and Paige Mortimer. And there—sitting all by themselves—were she and Stella. Two *friends*.

As Eleanor's clique erupted in laughter, Cate couldn't help but feel that maybe—just this once—Blythe had a point.

THERE'S NO SUCH THING AS AN UNPOPULAR MODEL

It was last-period study hall, and Lola had gotten through the entire day without being an awkward, clumsy twit. She'd woken up early to straighten her hair, and some eighth-year in gym had even told her it looked "hot." At lunch, she'd eaten strawberry frozen yogurt with Andie and her best friend, Cindy, and in orchestra she'd been given a viola solo in "Themes from the New World Symphony." For the first time since she got to New York, Ashton Prep was bearable.

Now she was in study hall, the girls around her hunched over their desks. A short brunette with too much eyeliner was reading *Pride and Prejudice* while another girl drew two sine curves on graph paper. Lola couldn't help thinking the sketch looked a little obscene, like a pair of knockers.

"Cookie?" the girl next to her asked, keeping her voice low. Technically, no one was allowed to talk during study hall. She offered Lola a plastic Tupperware container filled with lumpy cookies that looked greenish in the fluorescent light. "They're vegan."

Lola took a bite of one. "Mmmm," she said, pretending it didn't taste like cardboard. She only had two mates at Ashton Prep (if you counted Cindy)—she wasn't in a place to hurt anyone's feelings. "Thanks." In the front of the room Mr. McGregor, their study hall proctor, looked up from grading papers and put a finger to his lips.

"I'm Thea," the girl whispered. "You're in orchestra, right?" She had an auburn bob, and her blue button-down looked a few sizes too big. Lola recognized her from the cello section.

"Right," Lola choked down the bite of cookie. "I'm Lola. Andie Sloane's stepsister."

"I didn't realize that!" Thea cried, earning her another loud *shush* from Mr. McGregor. "I've known Andie since preschool." Lola smiled. She always felt more confident mentioning Andie when she introduced herself. Everyone knew who Andie was, and everyone seemed to like her.

"Our parents just got married," Lola added. She swallowed the last of the cookie, thankful it was gone.

"I noticed your necklace," Thea whispered. "Do you ride?"

Lola felt for the gold horseshoe charm around her neck. "I *did*. I had a horse back in London." She used to keep her palomino colt, Starlett, at Wimbleton Village Stables. She missed riding through the English countryside, looking out for the wild deer that always cut across their path. When they moved, they'd sold Starlett to a middle-aged man named Francis, who had red hair he wore in two braids, like Pippi Longstocking. Wherever Starlett was, wherever Francis was, she hoped he stroked her nose the way she liked and remembered to bring her brown sugar cubes. "I haven't been riding since last May, though."

"I ride horses in Prospect Park." Thea's hair fell in front of her face as she tucked the Tupperware container back into her SOY TO THE WORLD tote. "You should come sometime."

"That would be brilliant." Lola clapped her hands. She imagined riding a tree-lined bridle path, trotting alongside Thea on a brown-spotted Appaloosa. Soon they'd be hanging out at Thea's apartment after school, or writing notes to each other on their orchestra sheet music. Lola was certain she could come to like vegan cookies. And if she didn't, it was worth scarfing one down every once in a while if it meant she'd have a real friend in school—and one to go riding with.

Mr. McGregor turned on the telly in the corner of the room. Betsy Carmichael was already on screen, sitting at a table with the Ashton Prep crest behind it. She shuffled the stack of papers in her hand. "Good afternoon, ladies of Ashton Prep. I'm Betsy Carmichael, and this is your *Ashton News*."

As Thea and the rest of the study hall listened intently, Lola doodled a picture of Starlett on her notebook. Betsy kept on about the Ashton girls' soccer team, or how Shelley DeWitt had won first place in the six hundred at a track meet on Saturday.

"And now for the first-week-of-school highlight reel." Betsy's voice echoed in the room. Lola finished Starlett's tail, but the drawing looked a little like a German shepherd. Stella was always the one who was good at art.

Thea smacked her hand on Lola's desk, covering the drawing. "Look—it's Andie." Lola glanced up as the screen flashed a picture of Andie scoring a goal at last week's soccer game. The reel had been set to Pink's "So What," and it continued, showing a girl with dreadlocks jumping off the high dive. Then there was a clip of Cate and Stella at Jackson Hole with the Chi Beta Whatevers. And that's when it started: footage of Lola tripping in the street, her uniform skirt flying over her head to reveal her days-of-the-week knickers. Betsy had taken the video on the first day of school, and now it had been edited so that Lola fell over and over again, endlessly flashing the camera. The room broke out in laughter.

Lola adjusted her cloth headband, making sure it held down the tops of her ears. She wanted to throw her pencil at the screen, right between Betsy's big bug eyes. She already felt like Super Klutz of the Universe. She didn't need some ninth-year announcing it to the entire school.

"Who is that?" Thea asked, squinting at the telly like she needed glasses.

"I don't know," Lola lied. But a few of the girls in study hall had turned around, recognizing her. Lola had thought the footage had gone away, that Betsy would find a better story—bad mahimahi in the cafeteria or the librarian's stomach flu—to keep on about. But she was wrong.

Betsy looked directly into the camera and smiled. "And that, Ashton Prep, is your afternoon news. I'm Betsy Carmichael, signing off." She blew a kiss and the screen went black.

Thea glanced around as the rest of the girls filed out of the room, still giggling. A few turned back and pointed in Lola's direction. "I couldn't even tell it was you," Thea offered. "Want me to walk you home?"

Lola's nose twitched, the way it always did when she was about to cry. "That's all right," she said, not looking Thea in the eye. She wasn't about to be a bloody mess in front of someone she'd just met five minutes ago. And she could forget being friends with her now. "I just need a second."

"Okay . . ." Thea picked her bag up as if she were in slow motion. As she walked away, Lola could feel her eyes on her, but she refused to look up. Seeing the clips strung together like that it had been so bloody clear. Andie would always be the athletic sister. Cate and Stella would always be the popular sisters. And she would always be the klutz, with Dumbo ears and bowed legs, five inches taller than everyone else.

She sat alone and waited until the noise in the halls died down. She wouldn't go out there until everyone was gone *or* she was wearing a paper bag over her head. And she doubted Mr. McGregor kept a supply of them in his desk.

Ashton Prep made life in London seem easy. At Sherwood Academy, even the most popular bloke, Miles Conway, had helped her up the time she tripped over the roots of the old cherry tree in the schoolyard. Her best friend, Abby, brought an extra Scotch egg for her at lunch, and she'd been voted "Most Talented" in sixth year, for being the first-chair viola. But here it was useless. She could straighten her hair and wear some silly headband to hold down her ears—it wouldn't matter. She would never fit in.

As Lola picked herself out of the seat, she felt like she weighed thirty stone. She turned on her mobile, hoping her mum had called—or Abby—or anyone else she could actually talk to. There was one message.

A woman's voice spoke softly in her ear. "Hi, Lola. It's Ayana Bennington." It took Lola a moment to recognize the name. Ayana was an agent at Ford, and the first person (besides her mum) who'd ever told Lola she was pretty. According to Ayana, she wasn't bony—she had exquisite "bone structure." She wasn't too tall—she was "the perfect height" for runway modeling. "I'm calling because there's a casting this afternoon for Pacific Sunwear. I was hoping you'd be interested. Call me back at . . ."

Lola picked up her pen, copying down the number. When Ayana had said *Lola*—not Andie—was stunning, said *Lola*—not Andie—was high-fashion material, she'd never planned on doing anything about it. It was Andie's dream to be a model, not hers. But she hadn't planned on Betsy Carmichael showing that clip, either. For once, she just wanted to be like Cate or Stella or Andie—someone people didn't immediately roll their eyes at. Someone people looked up to . . . like a supermodel.

THE SECRET LIFE OF KYLE LEWIS

Andie took a deep breath, savoring the smell of freshly cut grass. She loved September, when the soccer fields in Central Park's North Meadow filled with high schoolers and the city cooled down just enough so you didn't break a sweat walking down the street. Andie sat on the sidelines, lacing up her dirt-caked cleats. On the opposite field, three Donalty girls practiced sprints, their glossy ponytails swinging back and forth as they ran.

Andie and her soccer team were having an informal scrimmage against the Haverford boys. They did it every Tuesday and spent the rest of the week gossiping about Jake Goldfarb asking Amanda Kowalsky to go to see *Wicked* with him, or speculating about why Austin Thorpe complimented Taylor Kline on her new shin guards. "What up, Sloaney Sloane?" Clay Calhoun called out as he walked toward the sidelines. He was the one Haverford boy everyone always talked about and swooned over, whether he did anything interesting or not.

He flung his Nike backpack to the ground and sat down next to Andie. He was wearing his bright blue Haverford mesh shorts, and his shaggy blond hair fell in his eyes.

"Not much," Andie mumbled, trying to force a smile. Clay had been flirting with her for the last year, after she'd stupidly agreed to go to the Haverford Middle School formal with him. He'd spent the entire time at the snack bar, making bets with his friends on who could eat the most bags of potato chips. When Andie danced with him, his breath smelled like a cheap barbecue restaurant.

"Yo—I just pantsed Brandon in Starbucks." Clay grinned as he took a bite of his banana PowerBar. With shaggy blond hair and perfect white *I never needed braces* teeth, all signs pointed to hottie. It was practically a rule in the Ashton Prep handbook: All middle school girls must have crushes on Clay Calhoun. But looking into his bright green eyes, Andie felt nothing.

"That's great . . ." She leaned over her shin guards to stretch. Clay was always rambling on about all the stupid things he and his best friend, Brandon O'Rourke, did. Just last week they stole Twizzlers from a deli on Eighty-sixth Street, and the week before that they drank two bottles of Coke and ate three bags of Pop Rocks, just to see if their stomachs would explode. They didn't.

Clay stopped chewing. "The barista totally saw his wiener."

Andie let out a small laugh. "That's crazy. Wasn't he wearing—"

"What are you up to Friday?" Clay interrupted. "Brandon and I are playing Ultimate Frisbee after school. We should hang out after." Behind him, Austin Thorpe, a starter for Haverford, passed out yellow and red jerseys. Everyone separated into coed teams.

"Umm . . ." Andie twisted her laces around her hand, turning her fingers a deep pink. She already saw Clay once a week—and that was one too many times. She was staring at a clover in the grass, trying to decide on a believable excuse (she had an eye doctor's appointment, she had to have dinner with Cindy's parents, she had to help Coach Higgins organize the sports closet) when she heard an unfamiliar voice.

"Andie!" From across the field, a boy with dark brown hair walked toward her. She shielded her eyes, just barely making out . . . Kyle Lewis. The last time she saw him—which was technically the first time she met him—she'd invited him to her dad's rehearsal dinner as her date. But she only did that to get back at Lola for stealing the spotlight during the meeting with Ford Models. Andie had always wanted to model, but Emma had been so busy with the wedding planning, there was never a good time to ask her about her new contract with Ralph Lauren, or how she'd met her first agent. So last week Lola had used her mom's name to get Andie an appointment at Ford, but it had been a complete disaster. The agent had asked *Lola* to come in for test shots. Andie had wanted to model, and Lola wanted to be Kyle Lewis's girlfriend. At the time, the trade-off seemed fair.

Of course, Andie had soon realized that Lola hadn't stolen her dreams at all—she revealed to Andie that she didn't even *want* to model. Now, Andie was thankful to have Lola as her stepsister. Maybe Lola was covered in orange cat hair, wore jeans that were an inch too short, and always tripped over her own feet. But she wasn't anything like Andie's older sister Cate. For one thing, it seemed like Lola actually *liked* spending time with her. And Andie could still pursue her dreams—maybe just a little more quietly. As soon as Emma returned from the honeymoon, Andie was planning on asking for her help. She'd waited a whole year to model—what was one more week?

"Who's that?" Clay muttered, pulling his cleats out of his knapsack.

Andie ignored him. "Kyle?" she asked, as he walked over to the sidelines. He looked adorable. The sleeves of his gray Donalty T-shirt were pushed over his shoulders, and the bridge of his nose was tan, like he'd stayed out in the sun just a little too long.

"Thanks for inviting me—this looks cool." He dug the toe of his cleat into the grass and looked around. By the goalpost, Taylor Kline warmed up by juggling the ball with her thighs.

Andie's mind raced. *What was he talking about?* Then suddenly she remembered: In the midst of her fighting with Lola, she'd invited Kyle to the scrimmage, too. Only she never thought he'd actually come . . . and Lola definitely didn't either. She'd cried when Andie had just *asked* Kyle to hang out. If she knew they were spending an afternoon together, she probably wouldn't get out of bed for a week. Andie tugged on the blond highlight in her bangs, which she did whenever she was nervous. *Lola can't find out about this,* she thought.

"Is there room for one more?" Kyle asked. He glanced at Clay, who was working at a knot in his laces with his teeth.

Kyle was standing on the field, wearing his shin guards and ready to play. They were on Ninety-seventh Street—she couldn't tell him to go all the way back to Tribeca now. And besides, it was only one soccer scrimmage—what was the harm in that? Andie looked into Kyle's warm brown eyes, the flecks of gold visible in the late afternoon sun. "Yeah," she heard herself say. "Definitely."

Two hours later, Central Park was still filled with people. A pack of bicyclists zoomed past, looking like speedy sea turtles in their kelly green Lycra suits and helmets. In the East Meadow, a man with a goatee played catch with his rottweiler, throwing around a suspiciously lifelike bone. A shirtless old man ran past Andie and Kyle, his sweat splattering everything within a two-foot radius around him.

They watched him disappear down the tree-lined path ahead of them as they continued walking. "Why is it always the oldest, saggiest, and sweatiest guys who don't wear shirts?" Kyle's smile revealed a dimple.

Andie laughed, but before she could answer, Clay appeared at the edge of the field, his shaggy blond hair sticking out in every direction. "Hey, Sloane, where you headed?" His white T-shirt had a big red stain on the front of it from when he'd poured a fruit punch Gatorade over his head in celebration.

"Gotta go," Andie called over her shoulder. "I'll see you next week!" She turned back to Kyle. Usually after every scrimmage Clay walked her home, but today she just couldn't listen to another word about Brandon O'Rourke's wiener.

"What about Friday?" Clay asked, but Andie just kept walking, pretending she didn't hear.

"We killed it," Kyle said, brushing his sweaty bangs off his forehead. "You were awesome." During their Tuesday scrimmages Andie was always quick on the field, determined to show the Haverford guys that she could hold her own. But today was different. She ran faster, her touch on the ball was perfect, and she didn't let a single player near their goalie. Having a new person watching her play made the game feel important, special, and every time she passed to Kyle she got an extra jolt of energy.

"Me? You're the one who scored three goals!" Andie twirled her ponytail around her finger. Before she met Kyle, she'd always assumed he was a massive dork. The Kyle Lewis that Lola talked about played the baritone horn, collected old Superman comic books, and had once tried to build a lunch box out of Legos. Even though she could tell right away he wasn't *that* high on the dork meter, for the first ten minutes of the scrimmage Andie had watched him nervously, afraid he might trip over himself or mention Kal-El or Krypton to Austin Thorpe. But after he nailed a corner kick—his second goal—it became clear that this Kyle Lewis was not the one Lola described. This Kyle Lewis was . . . cool. Even Jake Goldfarb, the other team's goalie, was impressed.

"Did you see Austin's face when you got the second one past him? He's not used to losing." Andie pushed her sleeves over her shoulder as they walked past the reservoir. She suddenly wished she were wearing her turquoise Elie Tahari silk dress instead of her old pit-stained Adidas T-shirt. She knew it was silly—she wore her soccer clothes more than she wore dresses. But this was the first time she was hanging out with Kyle, and she didn't want him to think she was a *complete* tomboy.

"I actually know Austin from Battle of the Bands." Kyle tugged at the gray sweatshirt tied around his waist.

"Wait—" Andie said, stopping in the middle of the gravel path. A three-year-old on a tricycle rode between them, pushing the pedals with great effort. "You played at Battle of the Bands? The one in June—at Arlene's Grocery?" Every year, Arlene's Grocery, a former bodega turned concert space, let the local high school kids compete for a chance to play at one of their Friday night shows. Usually Andie and her best friend, Cindy Ng, cheered for Austin's band, Nightlight Destroyers, even though their music sounded like screeching tires.

"Yeah, just the one for middle schoolers," Kyle said. "You've heard of it?"

Andie grabbed him. "I was there!" She looked at her hand on his arm, feeling her cheeks flush. She pulled it away and continued walking, keeping her eyes on the sidewalk. It was just too much of a coincidence. He'd probably been standing only a few feet away from her that very night. It was strange she hadn't realized it sooner. "Which band are you in?"

"The Wormholes?" Kyle asked, his cheeks a deep red.

"No way." She stared at him in shock, like he had just told her he spent last fall touring with Death Cab for Cutie. In June she and Cindy had not only seen the Wormholes, they had become obsessed with them, listening to their album *Spacetime* on repeat for five days straight. But she hadn't recognized Kyle at all. Suddenly it dawned on her: The lead singer K.L. always wore aviators and a headband, swinging his head back and forth to the music. "*You're* K.L.?" Andie felt goosebumps prickling up on her arms, something that only happened when she was freezing or insanely nervous.

"Yeah, it's kinda my band." Kyle laughed. He noticed Andie's goosebumped skin as they crossed Fifth Avenue. "Here—you look cold," he said, passing her his sweatshirt.

"Thanks," Andie managed. She wrapped it around her shoulders gratefully. Kyle Lewis, a.k.a. K.L., wasn't just the lead singer of the Wormholes—he was a minor celebrity at Ashton Prep. After the Battle of the Bands show, every seventh-grader started following the Wormholes on Twitter. Cindy had discovered "K.L."'s profile on Facebook, which said he was an eighth-grader at Donalty. Still, both of them were too embarrassed to actually friend him—they didn't want to seem like groupies.

"Uh . . . Andie? Isn't this your house?" Kyle had stopped against the wrought iron fence.

"Right." Andie had been so busy studying Kyle's face, trying to picture him in aviators and a headband, she hadn't realized where they were. She walked up to Kyle, close enough that she could see the tiny freckles that covered the tip of his nose. "Thanks for the sweatshirt," she said, pulling it from her shoulders.

"No, you can borrow it," he said, pointing to her bare arms, which still looked like a plucked chicken. "You're freezing."

"Thanks." She wrapped it around her shoulders and looked up into Kyle's brown eyes. She couldn't believe this was the same Kyle who, just three days ago, was standing in her foyer. "So I'll see you again next week?" *Say yes,* she thought, imagining them together every Tuesday, jogging around the reservoir and stopping for Pinkberry on their walk home. *Just say yes.*

"For sure." Kyle ran his thumb along the strap of his Adidas duffel bag. "But maybe we can talk before then—online?"

Andie tried to steady her voice. "Definitely. My screen name is Sloane28."

"Cool, I'll remember that." Kyle stepped out onto the sidewalk and smiled, a deep dimple in his right cheek. Then he took off toward Fifth Avenue, his bag swinging behind him. Andie pulled the sweatshirt off and held it in her hands, just staring at it. It was *Kyle Lewis's* sweatshirt. The same Kyle Lewis whom Lola had grown up with in London, skating in Hyde Park and playing Ghost in the Graveyard in their parents' gardens. The same Kyle Lewis Lola had gone to Madame Tussauds with just last week. And the same Kyle Lewis who was K.L.—the only boy who made Andie wish she went to Donalty.

It was wrong of her to think his dimples were adorable. Or that he was talented and sweet and all the things she wanted in a boyfriend. It was wrong of her to *like* him—but she couldn't stop herself. She hugged the sweatshirt to her chest, smiling as she breathed in a mixture of boy scent and Old Spice deodorant. If it was so wrong . . . why did it feel so *right*?

ONE OF THESE THINGS IS NOT LIKE
THE OTHERS

Later that afternoon, Lola stood in the poorly lit hallway of a building in SoHo, wearing her pink Speedo and a Gap white linen sundress. She stared at a door labeled PACIFIC SUNWEAR. The next time she was on *Ashton News*, she'd be in a Prada evening gown, strutting down the runway in Bryant Park, Betsy Carmichael running commentary on Ashton Prep's newest It girl (*Days-of-the-week knickers have been selling out all over the city! The fashion world speaks: Stop flattening your hair! Dumbo ears are so IN!*). The rag mags would finally have something to talk about other than her parents' divorce (*The Childs' Child Following in Mum's Footsteps!*), and Kyle Lewis, her childhood friend turned crush, would finally forget she was ever just his clumsy mate "Sticks."

She adjusted her cloth headband so that it held down the tops of her ears and entered the room, which smelled like a strange mixture of hair spray and baby oil. It was bustling with teenagers, all over the age of sixteen, and all looking like they had taken a break from surfing in Malibu to stop by the casting call. In the corner, a few girls examined themselves in Clinique compacts. Lola couldn't have gotten her skin that brown if she'd spent the entire summer roasting on a beach in Spain. The boys were uniformly handsome, reminding Lola of the small army of Ken dolls she had when she was little. Hearing the door shut, they all turned in unison like a herd of beautifully tanned, blond deer. Their blue eyes stared at Lola.

She pulled at the straps of her Speedo one-piece, realizing it probably wasn't *exactly* what Ayana had had in mind when she'd said "beachwear." She shifted around in her sundress, trying to cover the bright pink straps. "I'm here for the Pacific Sunset casting?" she said in a small voice.

Everyone was completely silent. "No way—did she just say Pacific *Sunset*?" a girl with a sunburned nose asked. She patted it with powder as she let out a loud cackle.

A pretty bloke with wavy, bleach blond hair eyed Lola's Speedo, which was still visible beneath her sundress, and her pale, freckled legs. He whispered to the bloke next to him. Then he turned to Lola. "Are you sure you're in the right place?"

Lola blushed so much her ears turned red. Everyone there had tiny button noses and golden brown skin, the color of chocolate chip cookies that had been in the oven just a little too long. None of them had bumps on their noses, none of them had skin so white you could practically see through it, and none of them had to wear a cloth headband just to pin back their bloody ears. "Maybe I made a mistake . . ." Lola mumbled, feeling for the door behind her.

As she turned quickly to leave, she felt her dress catch on the doorknob. There was a horrid ripping sound, then laughter. She felt a cool breeze on her legs and looked over her shoulder to see a piece of white linen hanging down, revealing her Speedo wedgie. She squeezed out of the room and flew down the staircase, not stopping until she was out on the street in the warm September air.

TO: Lola Childs
FROM: Ayana Bennington
DATE: Tuesday, 6:36 p.m.
SUBJECT: Pacific Sunwear casting call?
ATTACHMENT: Gutter and Light

Hi Lola,

I just heard from the Pacific Sunwear reps, who told me you failed to show up to the casting today. If I take the time to set up an appointment for you, I'd like you to take the time to actually go. I'm disappointed you missed it.

Assuming you're still interested in modeling, on Thursday I'd like you to meet with Gunther Gunta. He's in town for a few weeks looking for a new face for his next campaign. It's high fashion—but you're definitely in line with Gunther's aesthetic.

All the information is attached. It's essential that you be there. Gunther is extremely agitated by no-shows.

All the best,
Ayana

ASHES TO ASHES, DUST TO DUST, FROM NOW ON THEY'RE DEAD TO US

S tella sat in front of the fireplace in the living room on Tuesday night, working on a drawing of Heath Bar. He was curled up on the chaise lounge with her grandmum, who had fallen asleep reading her romance novel *Heating Up the Arctic*. The cover featured a man embracing a woman on the snowy tundra, his parka unzipped to reveal a shiny, waxed chest.

"Now don't move," she whispered to Heath Bar as she used the edge of her charcoal pencil to shade his fur. The giant tabby cat's eyes were half closed, his chin resting on his front paws. After the run-in with the Beta Sigma Phis today in gym, some relaxation time was just what Stella needed. She and Cate had spent the afternoon at Café d'Alsace, drinking cappuccinos and trying to figure out who was going to be the third member of their sorority. Cate had run down the short list: Celia Reynolds was sufficiently popular, but she didn't go anywhere without her best mate Benna Matthews. Benna wore Sally Hansen acrylic nails and sometimes spoke in a fake British accent, which would have driven Stella insane. Amy Klentak was cute and funny, and didn't belong to any one clique. But according to Cate, she had "major control issues." They could talk about Chi Sigma and plan as many bloody meet-and-greets as they wanted. It didn't matter. For now, it wasn't a sorority. It was just Cate and Stella.

"This is all of it!" Cate announced, strolling into the living room with a cardboard box. It was overflowing with old clothes, photos, and a poster that said CATE SLOANE FOR PRESIDENT. Seeing Cate, Heath Bar jumped off the chaise lounge and ran out the door, his back hunched in fear.

Stella put down her sketchbook and sighed. A blank circle stared out at her, right where the cat's face was supposed to be. Cate set the box down next to the fireplace and opened the grate. Then she began pulling items out with black iron tongs. "What is all that?" Stella asked.

"This," Cate said, stabbing at a black and white Nanette Lepore scoop-neck top and tossing it into the fire, "is the shirt Priya got me for my birthday last year." She watched as it burst into flames, the silk igniting instantly. "At least, it *was* the shirt Priya got me for my birthday last year. I'm purging."

"What?" Stella got up from the couch, her stomach tight. Cate was holding a stack of old pictures that looked like they had been taken over the last ten years. One was of her and Blythe dressed up as yellow chicks for Halloween. They looked about six. "You're not going to—"

But before she could go on, Cate threw all the pictures in the fire. A photo booth strip of the Chi Beta Phis curled and twisted, turning to ash. "It's the dawn of a new era. All this stuff is bad karma." She ripped the poster into pieces and threw that on the fire too. On the chaise lounge, Margot turned over in her sleep and coughed.

Cate picked up the old notes she and Sophie used to pass in seventh-grade health class (all folded into perfect footballs that read 4 UR EYES ONLY) and tossed them on the pile, feeling a little lighter. Over the last two hours she'd reread all the e-mails between her, Priya, and Blythe—the ones from fifth grade where they first planned the sorority. It had been Blythe's idea to name it Chi Beta Phi (Chi for Cate, Beta for Blythe, and Phi for Priya) and Cate who suggested they let Sophie in when she transferred to Ashton the following year. She'd shuffled through the postcards Blythe had sent her from Greece this summer, which were written in code so that Winston couldn't read them. Then she took out the cards from every one of her birthdays, the insides completely covered with writing. Every second of it was torture.

She didn't want to think about her friends. She didn't want to think about how Priya had helped her when she first got her period, stealing pads from the bottom drawer of her parents' bathroom. Or how Sophie had made flash cards for her when she was terrified she wasn't ready for the earth science final. She didn't want to think about how Blythe was the only person she felt comfortable enough to cry to—about Emma sleeping in her mom's room, or losing the sixth-grade election, or anything, really. She wanted all the memories to go away, to simply disappear. And this was the only way she knew how to make that happen.

She reached into the box and pulled out the last memory of

Chi Beta Phi: the Madame Alexander doll her friends had gotten her when she played Annie last year in Ashton's school play. They'd searched eBay for it for weeks, making sure to find one in mint condition.

"You're getting rid of *everything*?" Stella asked as she peered into the empty box. She felt like she had swallowed a handful of gravel. Yes, she was happy she and Cate were mates now and yes, she was happy Cate was finally free of Blythe's poisonous jealousy. But up until Stella moved to New York, the Chi Beta Phis were Cate's whole life. It would take all of high school and most of university before Stella and Cate had history like theirs.

"Chi Sigma needs to have a fresh start—if it's just you and me, it's just you and me. No baggage." Cate stroked the doll's hair and threw her onto the dwindling fire, along with her stuffed dog Sandy. Annie's glassy eyes stared at Stella as the flames died down around her. *You!* Stella imagined her screaming, *This is all your fault!*

Stella sat back down in Winston's leather club chair, determined. If she hadn't insisted on being in the Chi Beta Phis in the first place, none of this would've happened. She was the one who'd suggested the revote where Blythe had stolen Cate's presidency. Then she'd told the girls Cate had blabbed their secrets— that Blythe had a spray-tan addiction, Priya was obsessed with dissecting things at science camp, and Sophie still played with Barbies.

She pulled her sketchbook into her lap. As she scribbled furiously, Cate watched the last of the Chi Beta Phi memorabilia burn. Stella knew she had made a mess of Cate's ninth year. Now she was the one who'd clean it up. "What if," she started, "it wasn't just you and me? What if we were able to find the perfect third member?"

Cate shook her head, her shiny ponytail swinging back and forth. Kneeling in front of the fireplace in her pink plaid J. Crew pajamas, she looked like a small child. "How are we going to find a third member? We already went over our options—it's useless."

"We're not going to find a third member," Stella said, ripping a page out of her sketchbook and handing it to Cate. "*They're* going to find *us*."

CHI SIGMA [YOUR LETTER HERE]

Do you have what it takes to be in
Ashton Prep's hottest new sorority?

If so, come to the drawing room on Thursday
right after school and tell us why we should
choose you as our third member.

Bring your A-game, ladies—you're going
to need it.

*This once-in-a-lifetime opportunity brought to you
by Cate Sloane and Stella Childs.

"This is perfect!" Cate screamed. "We'll have the girls *rush*!" At this, Margot sat up, her thick blond hair falling in her eyes.

She looked around in confusion, like she wasn't sure if she was still dreaming.

Cate hugged Stella so tight she nearly cracked her ribs. News of the rush would spread faster than lice at a middle school sleepover. Girls would swarm Bergdorf's after school tomorrow, fighting over the perfect Badgley Mischka dress for their first impression. She pictured a line of ninth-graders outside the Ashton Prep drawing room, their résumés in hand as they rehearsed their Chi Sigma pitch. *I'm sorry, we need someone a little more . . . easygoing,* Cate imagined herself saying, as Amy Klentak threw a temper tantrum over her immediate dismissal.

"Good work," Cate said. As she looked at the flyer in her hands she imagined walking down the hall with her new sorority: Chi Sigma Theta, or Gamma, or whatever it became. It would never be Chi Beta Phi. Cate would never laugh as hard as she did when Blythe jokingly taped her nose up toward her forehead, making herself look like a pig. No one could comfort Cate as well as Priya, who was calmer than a yoga guru. And even Sophie was irreplaceable. Cate would always remember the "music video" she made on her webcam, where she lip-synched Fergie's "Glamorous" wearing every piece of her mom's diamond jewelry.

But Chi Beta Phi was over now. And if Cate and Stella's new sorority was going to be the best at Ashton Prep, it would have to be more visible, more popular, and fiercer than Blythe's. Cate clutched the flyer to her chest and smiled. She had put the Chi in Chi Beta Phi. She was *more* than up to the challenge.

IGNORANCE IS BLISS . . . AT LEAST
FOR LOLA

Andie carried the crumpet up the stairs, watching as the honey melted over its spongy top. She felt so guilty about hanging out with Kyle, she'd begged Greta, their cook, to make Lola's favorite snack. Kyle had IMed her yesterday, and they'd spent two hours debating the Shins vs. Death Cab for Cutie, and Killington vs. Sugarloaf. Afterward Andie rolled around in bed, unable to sleep. She couldn't stop picturing them huddled together on a ski lift, so close that Kyle's breath fogged up her goggles. It wasn't that she had a crush. It was that with every hour—every minute—it was getting worse.

She knocked on Lola's door. No matter how hard it was, no matter how mad Lola would be, she had to tell her—*now*. She only hoped the crumpets would serve as an adequate consolation prize.

"Look what Greta made!" she called out cheerfully. She set the plate down on Lola's dresser, right next to the framed picture of her and her best friend, Abby, on Primrose Hill. "Lola?"

"What?" a muffled voice said. It came from somewhere inside the mound of bedding piled on Lola's mattress. The tangle of pillows and blankets reminded Andie of the cushion forts she and Cate used to make when they were little, back when they could still stand to be in the same room together.

"Lola!" Andie cried, sitting down on the edge of the bed. She pushed back the patchwork quilt. Lola was curled up in a ball with her cheek resting on Heath Bar's furry back. Her eyes were swollen and red, like she'd had a severe allergy attack. Andie had seen the "first-week-of-school highlight reel" yesterday—it wasn't good. Lola had been on the verge of tears all through dinner last night. But eventually everyone ended up doing something stupid on *Ashton News*. It was like a rite of passage. Just last year they'd shown her getting knocked in the face with a soccer ball. "You cannot let Betsy Carmichael get to you. Besides, nobody cares if you wear days-of-the-week underwear."

"It's not that. Well, it's not *just* that." Lola stared at the turquoise wall and shook her head. The end of her freckled nose twitched, the way it always did when she was trying not to cry.

"What's wrong?" Andie leaned back, suddenly nervous. She'd waited a whole day to tell Lola she'd been talking to Kyle. She just hoped Kyle hadn't mentioned it first.

Lola sat up, sniffing back tears. "Everything," she mumbled, petting Heath Bar hard on his head. The tabby cat's eyes pulled back, like he'd just gotten a kitty face-lift. The highlight reel was only the beginning. All day, she couldn't stop thinking of how daft she'd been at the casting, or how she'd had to keep her hand on her dress for the entire tube ride home, so thirty more

43

people wouldn't see her bum. "It's not just the knickers thing, I—" She stopped herself. All last week Andie had kept on about Ford, striking impromptu poses in doors, puddles, and any other reflective surface she could find. Now Lola was the one going on casting calls. Even if she hadn't done anything wrong, it wasn't exactly the *easiest* news to share.

Lola let out a deep breath, feeling the words come out one by one. "That agent Ayana Bennington called me yesterday. I went on a modeling casting for some company called Pacific *Sunwear*." She made certain she said it right this time. Lola had only told her grandmum about the casting, and that was because she needed her to sign a release form. "I was daft to go. Everyone there was tan, with little ears and little button noses." Lola picked a piece of cat hair off the quilt, afraid to look up. "I'm sorry—I should have told you."

Andie stared at the horseshoe on Lola's wall. She didn't know what to say. After the incident at Ford, she'd told Lola it was okay with her if she wanted to model—she just hadn't thought Lola would go ahead and do it *two days later.* "It's fine . . . *really*," she managed. She pictured Lola going to the agency every day after school, passing Kate Moss in the lobby. *Lola!* Kate would cry, kissing her on both cheeks, *Let's get together after the Rodarte show!*

Still. She wasn't allowed to be mad. Not when she was scrimmaging with Kyle, talking to him online, and staying up late obsessing over what their first kiss would be like. Since Lola had kept her own secret, it was time for Andie to spill hers. "I've been meaning to tell you something."

"It's just," Lola interrupted, tears welling in her eyes, "I'm tired of feeling so . . . *ugly*." When she said the word *ugly* her chin wrinkled and she covered her face.

"You're not ugly!" Andie pulled Lola's hands away. All she could think was: Make Lola feel better. Now. "You're just not supposed to be modeling for Pacific Sunwear, that's all. Those girls are like Malibu Barbie dolls. You're more . . . *editorial*." Ever since Ayana had told Lola she was "stunning," Andie couldn't help noticing that Lola's freckled skin was flawless, or that she had an oddly delicate bump on the bridge of her nose. It was true—she had a unique look. Heath Bar walked over to Andie and started licking the back of her hand, his tongue scratchy like sandpaper.

"That's what Ayana said," Lola mumbled. "She's insisting I meet some bloke named Gunther Gunther tomorrow, but I just . . . I can't." Lola picked Heath Bar up and buried her face in his back.

"Gunther *Gunta*?"

"Yeah, that's it." Lola said. "You've heard of him?"

"*The* Gunther Gunta?" Andie was stunned. Gunther Gunta was number one on Andie's list of Designers to Work With, ahead of Marc Jacobs and Vera Wang. For her twelfth birthday she'd begged her dad to buy her a Gunther Gunta vintage couture dress, even though it was only appropriate for the Oscars, the Emmys, or a runway in Milan. After Winston's tailor made some serious alterations, she spent a whole week wearing it around the house, practicing her runway walk in wedge heels. "Lola—do you have any idea who that is? You have to go!"

Andie grabbed last month's *Vogue* off Lola's nightstand. It was in the same exact spot she'd left it last week, when she was trying to school Lola about fashion. She opened to a spread titled "Gunther Gunta: Man. Myth. Maniac?" and pressed her finger into the page. "He's a fashion icon—bigger than Calvin Klein, Karl Lagerfeld, Versace. He's Indian, but he was born in Paris and moved to Germany when he was three. People claim he was designing dresses before he could talk, fashioning scarves out of his baby blankets. His first fashion show was in Munich when he was only seven." Andie looked at a photo of the young Gunther watching his own fashion show and smiled. Even as a kid he had glasses an inch thick, his red beret sitting lopsided on his head.

Lola looked at the spread. In the center there was a blurry paparazzi shot of a short man lying out by a pool, his hairy gut hanging over his Speedo. A newspaper covered his face. "*That's* him?"

"He's been in seclusion for the last two years—that's the only recent picture they have." Andie tried not to sound so annoyed. Lola didn't know Armani from Arkansas, and she was meeting *Gunther Gunta* tomorrow. It wasn't fair. Andie had watched footage of his early fashion shows and read every article about the alleged breakdown that put him in seclusion. Two weeks after critics called his fall 2007 collection "an utter abomination," Gunther disappeared. He was discovered a month later lying in an alley in Paris, muttering to himself as he gnawed on the end of a stale baguette. Andie had read so much about Gunther, seen so many interviews, she felt like they were friends. She'd even rehearsed what she would say if she met him: *Don't listen to the critics! Your fall 2007 collection was* an utter inspiration.

"You have a big day tomorrow. I should let you rest up." Andie headed toward the door. She felt confused, like when she'd found out Cindy—her always prudish best friend—had kissed a boy before she had. Lola was supposed to be the sister who *didn't* intimidate her.

"Wait—didn't you want to tell me something?" Lola asked. The quilt was thrown over her shoulders, like an ugly patchwork shawl.

Andie eyed the crumpet on Lola's dresser, remembering why she had come there in the first place. She was talking to Kyle Lewis—*Lola's* crush. "Just . . ." She looked at Lola's face, which was still pink and swollen. Whether Lola was modeling for Gunther Gunta or not, Andie knew the moment she left, Lola would bury her head back in the blanket. "Don't worry. You're perfect for modeling. Gunther will love you."

Lola smiled, revealing a small glimpse of her usual, enthusiastic self. "Cheers," she whispered, pulling Heath Bar into her arms. And with that, Andie left.

TO: Andie Sloane
FROM: Kyle Lewis
DATE: Wednesday, 6:02 p.m.
SUBJECT: Hey there

Signed on but you're not here. Anyway, here are the links for those YouTube videos I was talking about. I can't stop laughing at that one with the pit bull break dancing.

Kyle

PS: You were right about that Decemberists song—the acoustic version of "Engine Driver" is so much better.

TO: Kyle Lewis
FROM: Andie Sloane
DATE: Wednesday, 7:11 p.m.
SUBJECT: Re: Hey there

Hilarious video. This totally made my night. This
week is turning out to be kind of . . . weird (long
story). I'll definitely talk to you soon. Can't wait.

XOXO
Andie

ASHTON PREP GIRLS DO THEIR HOMEWORK

Cate leaned on the wrought iron fence outside her town house, glancing every so often at her Tiffany Crown of Hearts watch. All day, girls had been peppering her with questions, asking if there would be a talent portion of the audition, or if she preferred they change out of their uniforms and into a specific designer label. Everything was as it was supposed to be: Girls were back to looking to Cate for advice, and Chi Sigma was already on its way to beating out Beta Sigma Chi as the most popular sorority at Ashton Prep. But if she was going to make ninth grade her defining year, she was still missing one key ingredient: a boyfriend. And that's where Eli Punch came in.

Danny Plimpton dashed down Eighty-second Street. His red and blue–striped tie was blown over his shoulder, like he'd just stepped out of a wind tunnel. "It's about time," Cate hissed, snatching the lime green folder from his hands.

"It wasn't my fault!" Danny had thick black eyebrows and a nose that turned up at the end. He reminded Cate of the Grinch

Who Stole Christmas. "Mr. Klotchske gave me detention for spitting on the sidewalk."

"Save it." Cate turned the folder over in her hands. The front of it had a picture of a stick figure planting a tree, the words THE GREEN CLUB printed right above it. Two whole days had gone by since she first met Eli, and she still hadn't had one real conversation with him, unless you counted his original "hi." Still, she found herself sitting up straighter in class, smiling as she walked down Madison Avenue, and spending twenty extra minutes picking out her uniform shirt. She felt an imaginary set of eyes on her all the time—*Eli's* eyes. She was starting to feel like the lovesick Eponine in *Les Misérables,* always pretending Marius was beside her. She didn't just want to be Eli's girlfriend. He made her want to be a better version of herself.

She opened the folder slowly, breathing in the cool night air. Eli Punch's smiling face looked directly at her. She smiled back.

"It's everything from the last two days, just like you asked." Danny tugged on the ends of his tie. His uniform shirt was untucked, his tiny legs sticking out underneath it.

This was it. The crucial piece of the Eli puzzle—his life at Haverford. Cate thumbed through the materials, which included Eli's schedule, napkins and receipts Danny had scribbled on (*the Eagle wiped his mouth with this at lunch; receipt from the Eagle's recent Coke purchase*), and candid photos Danny had taken on his iPhone. There was one of Eli eating turkey burgers with Braden Pennyworth, Haverford's star basketball player, and one of him in his Brooks Brothers boxers and a T-shirt that looked like it had been taken from the inside of a locker. In the last one he was wearing the Haverford signature red and blue shorts, a basketball tucked under his arm. "Wait—he's on the Haverford varsity team?"

"Yup." Danny glanced inside the front window. He was three inches shorter than Lola and could've easily been mistaken for a fourth-grader.

Cate pressed the photo to her chest. "And he's only a sophomore," she said. The only thing better than having a Haverford boyfriend was having a Haverford boyfriend on the varsity basketball team. Every Ashton Prep girl was part of the Facebook group "Waiting for Braden Pennyworth to be single again" or "I don't really like basketball but those Haverford jerseys are hot." Betsy Carmichael even had a special segment on the *Ashton News* where she named members of the team M.A.P.s (Most Adorable Players).

"Good work," Cate said, digging through her black and white Balenciaga bag. She pulled out a picture of Lola and one of her friends on Hampstead Heath in London. Cate had plucked it from her bulletin board that afternoon. Lola was wearing shorts that came down past her knees, and her fried hair was tucked behind her huge ears. Lola was more awkward than a fart in an elevator. It was kind of amazing that someone had a crush on her. "Try not to slobber all over it. I'm also ninety-nine percent certain she does not have a date to the Haverford formal."

Danny shoved it in his backpack. "Thanks." He smiled, pushing his dark curls out of his eyes. "Eli should be here in five minutes. He was just leaving the locker room when I saw him." Then he took off down the street, leaving Cate to her research.

According to the folder, Eli ate a turkey burger with Swiss every day at lunch, always kept the top button of his shirt unbuttoned, and had been spotted hanging out on the grass outside the Museum of Natural History after school. He had three basketball games in the next two weeks, he wasn't good at long division, he bought his socks at American Apparel, and he might need glasses (*the Eagle seen squinting at the blackboard*).

Cate smoothed down the skirt of her Diane von Furstenberg chiffon dress. Stella had helped her pick it out after dinner, saying she'd worn something similar when she went to the movies with her sixth-grade boyfriend. Whenever Stella brought up boys, Cate tried her best to keep up, offering the occasional *I so know what you mean,* or *totally!* But the truth was, she so *didn't* know what Stella meant. Cate had spent every second of middle school with the Chi Beta Phis, planning brunches at L'Absinthe and picnics by the Turtle Pond. Every Valentine's Day Cate exchanged gifts with Blythe, Priya, and Sophie, making them cheesy doily paper cards. She hadn't even gotten her first kiss until this past summer. Now she was fourteen, Chi Beta Phi–less, and playing a serious game of catch-up. While everyone else was sprinting toward second dates, serious boyfriends, and hookups, Cate was still at the starting line, trying to figure out when the gun went off.

Across the street, Mrs. Ashford watered her window boxes, singing to her mums like they were small children. Cate let out a deep breath as a boy turned down Eighty-second Street. It was Eli—she recognized him immediately. He was still in his Haverford warm-ups, his blue pants making a swishing sound as he walked.

She'd had this conversation in her head a thousand times in the last two days, when she was brushing her teeth, blow-drying her hair, and in the last moments before she fell asleep. She imagined bumping into Eli on the crosstown bus, or catching him peering over the roof deck wall at her, as she lay out in her Theory bikini. *You live next door—right?* she'd casually say, shooting him her most flirtatious, *I haven't been stalking you* smile. But now that he was actually here, walking toward her—in real life—her mouth felt dry, like she'd just eaten an entire box of saltines.

Eli pushed his thick black hair off his forehead and looked up at Cate's town house. "What's up . . . *neighbor?*" He let out a little laugh.

"Hey." Cate held on to the wrought iron fence, steadying herself. "Yeah, I meant to introduce myself the other day. I'm Cate—Cate Sloane."

"I'm Eli. I would shake hands, but I'm a little sweaty." Cate studied him as he ran his thumbs along the straps of his backpack. His dark eyes were surrounded by a thick curtain of black lashes, and he was the three T's that Ashton girls always used when classifying the Haverford basketball team: tall, tan, and toned. "I just moved this weekend, from Connecticut."

I know, Cate thought. After Danny gave her the first batch of intel, she'd Googled Westport and found out Eli had run a 5K there, finishing in an impressive 20:34. She discovered an old camp photo of him on a sailboat and an article on deer he'd written for the school paper. Even if he'd only spoken twenty-two words to her, she was starting to feel like she knew him better than anyone else. "How do you like New York so far?"

Eli smirked, his lips twisting like he'd just licked a lemon. "Well . . . I still don't instinctively know which way is uptown and which way is downtown like everyone else seems to, and this morning some cabbie tried to make me roadkill." He rested his foot on the fence, his leg just inches away from Cate's.

Mrs. Ashford turned away from her mums and raised an eyebrow at Cate. She had been friends with Cate's mother and felt that entitled her to eavesdrop on all Cate's conversations. Cate shot her an evil glare and turned back to Eli.

"Well, if you need any help, I'm right next door." She imagined taking the 6 train downtown with Eli, pressed close together in the crowded subway car. They'd walk arm in arm around the über-modern Whitney Museum and giggle as they tried to figure out how a plain red canvas made "art." Cate couldn't wait for Blythe, Priya, and Sophie to spot them holding hands on Madison Avenue, or sharing a kiss in Bergdorf's. It would be official proof that Cate was over the Chi Beta Phis. She could finally stop thinking about how Sophie's birthday was coming up in October, or how Priya's parents were taking her to India in December, and move onto bigger and better—not to mention cuter and cuddlier—things.

"I could use a personal tour guide . . ." Eli said, emphasizing the word *personal*. Cate twisted her dark brown hair into a ponytail and smiled. She would do anything to have five hours alone with Eli, even if it meant walking Manhattan from the Hudson to the East River. "I'll take you up on that." Then he started up his stoop.

Cate watched him go, her hand gripping the fence. She

couldn't hold a stake out every night, hoping he'd walk by. She needed a goal, a plan, so she could stop *imagining* hanging out with him and start *actually* hanging out with him. "Maybe I'll check out one of your basketball games sometime?" she called after him. She'd already looked at the schedule.

Eli paused on the top step and put his key in the door. "Yeah, there's one tomorrow. You should come," He smiled, then disappeared inside.

"*You should come,*" Cate whispered to herself. She held the folder to her chest, her heart pounding like she'd just run ten blocks. Tomorrow Eli would scan the stands and see her sitting there, her hair straightened, lips glossed, cheering him on. By Friday they'd be sitting in the Rose Planetarium in the dark, huddled together under a fake sky of stars. And next week she'd be lying out on the Great Lawn after school, using his chest as a pillow. Forget the fitted vest—Eli Punch was the hottest new fall accessory.

SHARING IS CARING

Stella winced as Myra Granberry plunged the scalpel into the pig's heart, half expecting to get squirted in the eye with formaldehyde. She'd been stuck with Myra as a lab partner ever since her first day at Ashton Prep, when Cate banned her from the Chi Beta Phis. Myra was brilliant at biology and genuinely nice, but standing next to her made Stella a nerd by association. Myra had a clunky mobile that she clipped to her uniform skirt, was the star of the Mathletes, and fancied using words like *golly* and *gosh*.

"The first cut should be vertically down the center." Mrs. Perkins, their just-out-of-grad-school biology teacher, drew a line over the diagram of the heart taped to the board. Whenever she raised her arms too high, her Ann Taylor cardigan rode up, exposing her Celtic lower-back tattoo. Around the room, girls hovered over their dissection trays. Analeigh Price, the girl who'd declared herself an "animal lover" before class, choked back tears as she made the first cut.

Just then Priya strolled in, whispering an apology to Mrs. Perkins. Her curly black hair was pulled back in a loose bun, and the collar of her pink Ben Sherman button-down was popped up. She made a beeline to Stella's lab table, clutching a lavender flyer in her hand. Stella recognized it immediately.

"Just when I thought this couldn't get any more ridiculous. Now you're *advertising* for friends?" Priya shook her head as she set the flyer down in front of Stella. Her black eyes were lined with silver shadow, making them sparkle.

Stella scraped her nails along the wooden stool. She'd never had to advertise for friends before—ever. In London she, Pippa, and Bridget were invited to every party and every cricket match, cheering as their mate Robin Lawrence ran between wickets. After they started having tea at the Ritz on Saturday afternoons, the entire school showed up, ordering the same carrot cake Stella loved. Last fall a fifth-year had even started a blog, showing girls which shops carried the designer samples Stella inherited from her mum. But in Manhattan—at Ashton—she was a bloody pariah.

Stella was tired of waiting for classes with Cate to have a decent conversation with someone, tired of getting points off her English papers for spelling color *colour* or center *centre*, and most important, she was tired of the Beta Sigma Phis treating her like some poor, desperate loner.

She glanced at Myra, who was now cutting at the heart sideways, licking her lips in concentration like it was a juicy slab of Kobe beef. Stella grabbed the tray from her and shoved it into Priya's arms, knocking her in the ribs. "Here—I know how much you love dissecting things."

Priya backed away. "No, I'll leave that to you and your"—she smirked, eyeing Myra—"*friend.*" She retreated to a table on the other side of the classroom, where Sophie was watching everything. As Priya put on her latex gloves, Sophie snuck a small wave.

Stella couldn't help but smile. Sometimes she felt like Sophie was the real victim in all of this. Just yesterday, she'd ambushed Stella in the gym loo. *I'm sorry!* she'd whispered under the stall. *I just want us all to be friends again!*

"What did she mean—*advertise*?" Myra asked. Her gloves were covered with pink fluid, so she was trying to scratch her nose with her arm.

"It's just . . . Cate and I got into a huge fight with Blythe, Priya, and Sophie." Stella put on her latex gloves and held the tray steady. "Now we're forming our own sorority, and we're looking for a third member. It's a long story. Basically they were mad that I lied about some things." Even now, Stella couldn't believe how angry they'd gotten. What was she supposed to do, say *Hi, nice to meet you, my dad cheated on my mum with Cloud McClean? You know, that British pop singing twit with the new line of glitter thongs?* Before last week, she'd only told two people outside of her family about Cloud: Pippa and Bridget. It wasn't the type of thing you sent a mass e-mail about.

"What kinds of things?" Myra pressed. As she leaned over the tray, strands of white blond hair fell in her eyes. She wore a short-sleeved cotton turtleneck, the Ashton Prep crest pinned to the collar.

Myra Granberry was, quite possibly, the only person in the

world Stella could tell about Cloud without worrying the rumors would spread like chicken pox. At the very worst, she would only repeat it to their geometry teacher, Miss Katz, or her pet sea monkeys. She didn't talk to anyone else—or rather, no one else talked to her. "Do you know who Cloud McClean is?"

"Is she that eleventh-grader with the blue hair?" Myra asked, her brown eyes wide.

Stella laughed, but Myra kept looking at her. She had a bleached white mustache, and her nearly invisible brows were furrowed in confusion. Stella had never met anyone who didn't know who Cloud McClean was. It seemed like her song "Kick It" was playing on every radio station, that that silly advertisement of her eating lollipops was in every tube station, and that her line of glitter thongs was in every store, perched right next to the cash register. "No, not quite. . . . She's a pop singer. They were mad I was keeping a secret from them about my dad. . . ." Stella glanced around the room, lowering her voice so only Myra could hear. "He cheated on my mum with her."

Myra dropped the knife on the dissection tray, making a loud metallic *clink!* The entire room turned. "Oh my gosh," Myra hissed. She looked around and leaned in close, lowering her voice. "I'm so sorry."

"Right, thanks." Stella felt her cheeks flush. Nobody had ever apologized for her dad cheating on her mum. Pippa and Bridget hadn't a bloody clue what to say when she told them—they mostly stared at their hands. Her mum had spent a week in her bedroom with the curtains drawn and her dad, Duke "Toddy" Childs, had apologized that "they had to go through this," or said he was sorry that "this had happened." He made it sound like an earthquake, a perfect eight on the Richter scale, had destroyed their home and there was simply nothing he could've done about it.

After her parents told her about the divorce, Stella walked around their neighborhood alone, blaming the cold winter air for the tears in her eyes. She'd passed her house on Cheyne Walk three times, circling the block and wishing any other place was hers. She wanted to go back inside and have it be the summer again, when her family was celebrating Lola's eleventh birthday in the garden. Before Cloud ever met her dad. Before things went wrong.

"It's just—that's really awful." Myra's brown eyes looked wet. She held a latex glove to her heart, like she was about to say the Pledge of Allegiance. A tiny bit of pale pink liquid stained her shirt.

Stella turned away, trying to avoid Myra's gaze. "I'm fine, really." Compared to Lola, she was. Lola hadn't talked to their dad since last winter. Every time he called her mobile, she sent it straight to voice mail. Before they left for New York, the three of them had eaten dinner at Pasha, the Turkish restaurant Lola had always loved. Lola played the mute card and refused to speak, even after their dad gave her a Burberry cat carrier for Heath Bar. He'd finally gotten so frustrated he'd canceled their dessert order.

"I kind of understand," Myra continued. "My mom remarried a few years ago. It's just me and my dad. He invented the under-water flashlight?"

Myra waited for Stella to respond. She nodded as if to say, *Oh yes! The underwater flashlight!* Myra smiled, looking even happier than she had yesterday when Mrs. Perkins announced they were dissecting pig hearts. She was starting to make sense—the striped rainbow knee-highs she wore under her uniform skirt, her barely visible eyebrows, or the way her part was always crooked (and not in a cool, intentional way). Most mums would've broken out the home waxing kit before sending their daughter out of the house with a bleach blond mustache. Even if your dad *did* invent the underwater flashlight, or the underwater hair dryer, microwave, and popcorn maker—there were some things men just couldn't do.

"Anyway," Myra continued, cutting back into the pig heart. "What do you think my chances are?"

Stella glanced around the room, which smelled of formaldehyde and bleach. Analeigh Price watched in horror as her lab partner picked the heart up, making it "dance." Mrs. Perkins was sitting cross-legged on the corner of her desk, reapplying her lipstick. "Chances of what?" Stella asked, confused.

"Of making it into your sorority?" Myra pulled off her gloves. The heart was pinned open on the wax tray.

Stella tried to smile, but her skin felt as hard as plastic. Statistically speaking, Myra's chances were not even point one percent of point one percent. Cate would rather let Heath Bar use her Balenciaga bag as a litter box than let Myra Granberry, Mathlete president and proud owner of a ferret named Pythagoras, into Chi Sigma.

Stella looked down at the heart. She imagined a depressed

Myra eating a frozen dinner at her kitchen table, lit up by a single exposed lightbulb. Her father would keep on about the inner workings of his newest invention, pausing every so often to drop some crumbs to Pythagoras. "You have as good a chance as everyone else," she offered.

"Gosh," Myra said, clasping her hands together. "Thanks!" She enveloped Stella in a hug, squeezing her tightly.

Stella closed her eyes and hoped Cate would never find out she'd extended the invite. But more than that, Stella hoped Myra would have a last-minute Mathlete meeting, a sudden cold, or a cousin in on a surprise visit from Albuquerque—anything that would keep her from actually showing up.

TO: Cate Sloane
FROM: Blythe Finley
DATE: Wednesday, 7:22 p.m.
SUBJECT: Desperate much?

Saw your flyer around school today. I heard Liza Bartuzzo (you know, the head of the marching band flag twirlers?) was particularly excited about the open call. You've really given all the Ashton underlings something to strive for.

I'm off to Sophie's now—Beta Sigma Phi is having its first midweek sleepover. Good luck sorting through our leftovers.

Blythe
Blythe Finley
President of Beta Sigma Phi

"With great power comes great responsibility." —F.D.R.

TO: Blythe Finley
FROM: Cate Sloane
DATE: Wednesday, 7:26 p.m.
SUBJECT: Missing me much?

Dearest Blythe,

I know this is hard for you. And I know these
e-mails are just your lame attempt to talk to me.
You're lonely, I can tell. Who can blame you? No one
knows how you're surviving, now that you have no
one to give you a constant stream of fashion advice,
or decide what you're going to eat for lunch.

I can't really e-mail, though—Stella and I have to
finish planning the open call, and I have to decide
what I'm going to wear tomorrow. Eli invited me to his
game (you know, Eli Punch? The newest member of
the Haverford varsity basketball team?).

Cate Sloane
Co-president of Chi Sigma

CHI SIGMA ... ALPHA?

Andie hit the shuttle with her racquet, sending it soaring over the net. It was Thursday morning gym class, and Mrs. Taft had paired her off with Hannah Marcus. Andie had always hated badminton. It was like a lame version of tennis, for people who were over seventy-five or just plain lazy. Hannah fell into the second category. Playing with her was like playing with a statue—she refused to move even six inches to keep the game going.

Hannah swung her racquet and missed, the shuttle falling a few feet to the right of her feet. Andie gazed longingly at Cindy, who was running around the corner court, having a quick back-and-forth with Addison Isaacs. "So," Hannah said, as she walked to retrieve the shuttle. She was moving so slowly, it was like she was stuck in mud. "It seems like Cate is coping okay without Blythe." When she bent over, her purple tank top rode up, revealing her chubby back.

"Yeah," Andie offered. She had heard that Cate and Blythe

weren't friends anymore—*everyone* had heard. "She's great." The truth was, most girls at Ashton Prep—even ones Cate *wasn't* friends with—were better qualified to answer that question than Andie. Hannah gave the shuttle a halfhearted whack and Andie smashed it right back. It bounced off the shiny gym floor, not going anywhere near Hannah's racquet.

Andie and Cate were close when they were younger, before their mother died. They'd throw birthday parties for Andie's American Doll, Molly—even wrapping up Winston's Tiffany cuff links as a gift. They'd put on elaborate plays in the den and borrow their mother's pearls and diamond brooches to pretend they were princesses, trapped in an ogre's castle. And when their mom was really sick, it was Cate who had worn one of her wigs, pretending it was just another play so Andie wouldn't be so scared. But it hadn't been like that in years.

Hannah huffed to the far corner of the badminton court and served the shuttle back over the net. "Everyone's talking about the rush. A few girls stole some flyers from the upper school."

"What do you mean?" Andie caught the shuttle in her hand and just held it there.

"*Do not* tell me you haven't heard." Hannah's brown hair was a mess of frizzy curls, and she had a mole on her chin the size of a pencil eraser. Cindy only referred to her as "Holy Mole-y." She dropped her racquet to her side, like she'd given up on the game completely. "She and Stella are having an open call today to find a third member for Chi Sigma."

Andie tugged on the highlight in her bangs. She knew Chi Beta Phi was done. But she didn't know Cate and Stella were starting their *own* sorority . . . and looking for one more member. Over the last few years, there hadn't been any space in Cate's life for her. Every weekend Cate was holed up in her room with "her real sisters," the Chi Beta Phis, watching marathons of *The City* and singing all three hundred songs on her karaoke machine. Andie used to listen to them through the heating vent in her bathroom, wishing, just for once, they'd ask her to join. "When is it?" Andie asked.

"After school. I just assumed you were going." Hannah started to sit down on the court, but Mrs. Taft blew her whistle, bringing her to attention.

"Back to the game, Hannah, period's almost over," she called. She was standing next to the gymnasium doors with her clipboard. Her thick legs were packed into gray Ashton Prep sweatpants, making them look like Polish sausages.

"I mean, you're the most obvious third member," Hannah continued, as Andie served back to her. "You *are* related to them." She looked at Hannah's pale face and decided, right then, that she was more likeable than people gave her credit for.

"Maybe I will go." She and Cate always got along on vacation, when Cate's only choices were to hang out with Andie or be alone. Last winter in Killington, Cate had jumped out of the hot tub on Andie's dare, rolling around in the snow until her skin was pink. In Australia they'd snorkeled side by side over the Great Barrier Reef, gripping each other's hands because they were so terrified of sharks. Andie wanted *that* Cate to be her sister—the one who could go more than an hour without snapping at her, or slamming a door in her face. To Andie, those vacations always felt like proof that they could get along. Cate just had to be willing to give her a chance.

"All right, ladies," Mrs. Taft called out, nodding to the locker room doors. "I'm done torturing you." As Andie dropped her racquet into a giant red bin, Hannah pulled a lavender sheet of paper out of her flowered LeSportsac. She offered it to Andie. "Here, I found an extra one in the courtyard. It's yours if you want it."

Andie turned it over in her hands. "Thanks, Hannah." The girls filed inside the locker room, but Andie lingered behind. She imagined walking to school with Cate and Stella, stopping for café lattes at the Starbucks on Eighty-seventh Street. Cate would review her schedule for her in June, telling her which teachers to avoid and why, and look over all her papers on *A Christmas Carol* or *Huck Finn*. They'd all stay up late, having their *own* karaoke sleepover. Andie would do her best rendition of "Girls Just Wanna Have Fun," and they wouldn't care that she was completely tone deaf.

She tucked the flyer into her pocket and headed inside, the slightest smile creeping over her face. Finally she wouldn't be Copy Cate, or C.C., the annoying cling-on that Cate was always trying to get rid of.

THE ROAD TO THE TOP IS PAVED WITH FAT LITTLE MEN

When the lift doors opened into the Royal Suite in the Waldorf Towers, Lola clapped her hands in excitement. Its eighteenth-century antiques and gilded crown molding made her feel like she'd walked into a life-size dollhouse. The pink and turquoise damask curtains were pulled back to reveal a spectacular view of Central Park, the high-rise buildings around it sparkling in the afternoon sun. "New York Sit-aaaay," Lola whispered, her lips curling into a smile. It was awful how much she missed London, with its quaint little streets and alleyways, but at a time like this, it was impossible to be sad. Here she was, in a posh hotel, about to meet Gunther Gunta, world-famous fashion designer.

Two models sat on gilt wood settees, barely looking up as Lola entered. A young girl flipped through a *Vanity Fair* that had Lola's mum's friend, the British actor Harley Cross, on the cover. Lola studied the girl, a little relieved. She had skin so white she looked albino, and her red hair was the color of fire

chance." Lola wrung her hands. The last thing she needed was Gunther Gunta: Man. Myth. Maniac? pulling off her headband and telling her she had elephant ears, or demanding she bleach away her freckles. She took a deep breath, remembering Andie's words. *You're editorial. Gunther will love you.* Lola hoped she was right.

She opened the heavy oak door. The dining room had been cleared of furniture and the thick curtains were drawn. It was dark except for a single spotlight that lit up the wall, like a perfect glowing moon. "Stend on ze X," a low voice hissed. It was coming from the far end of the room, where two shadowy figures sat in armchairs. Lola couldn't quite make out their faces. "Do nut speek," the man said.

"Donut speak?" Lola furrowed her brows, imagining two chocolate Krispy Kremes talking to each other. She stepped onto the masking tape X on the floor and smoothed down the skirt of the black Gap chiffon dress she'd bought for her uncle Simon's wedding last year. Andie had helped her pick it out, insisting it was the outfit most "in line with Gunther's sensibilities."

"Shhhh!" the voice hissed. The spotlight was so bright it was like staring directly at the sun. Lola shielded her eyes, trying to make out who was talking. "Lit me zee your face!"

Lola braced herself, waiting for Gunther to sling his first insult. He would tell her to get knee-reduction surgery, to break her feet so they didn't turn inward so much, or to splurge on fat injections for her arms. He would scrunch his nose in disgust, insulted she'd even come. Lola waited. The sweat pooled at the small of her back. There was only silence.

In the back of the room she saw the flame of a lighter, then the glow of a freshly lit cigarette. Lola coughed, the smoke stinging her throat. She wanted to run out the door, down the ornate hallways of the Waldorf Towers, and up Park Avenue, not stopping until she was at home with Heath Bar, cuddled safe in her bed. She'd been so dim. Gunther Gunta was looking for a high-fashion model, not some twit who couldn't walk to the loo without falling over her own feet. "Um . . ." Lola mumbled, staring at the carpet. "I'm sorry for wasting your time. I'll—"

"No!" The man's voice growled. "Evette. Ze lights!" He snapped his fingers in the air. The shadow with the cigarette walked over and flipped a switch on the wall.

Lola blinked a few times, the room slowly coming into focus. There was an oak credenza next to her, decorated with two ivy topiaries. The woman on the far wall wore high-waisted pants and a blue beret and was enveloped in a cloud of smoke. She reminded Lola of the women in those subtitled films her mum liked to watch. Then Lola spotted him.

Walking toward her was a round man just a little taller than Andie. His hair formed one stiff black peak, like it had been gelled back with rubber cement. In his striped blue T-shirt and jeans he looked a little like the street performers in Covent Garden, only older . . . and fatter. And he wasn't juggling bowling pins.

He circled Lola three times, peering up at her through his Prada glasses. They were half an inch thick, making his black eyes look as tiny as peas. "Git rid of eet!" he hissed, snapping his fingers at Lola's headband.

Lola had barely taken it off since last week, when she bought it at some place called Duane Reade, which Andie had explained was New York City's version of Boots. The headband held down the tops of her ears. Now that she had it, it wasn't something she could do without. "Um . . . I'd rather—"

"Ne-ow!" Gunther hooted, throwing his short arms in the air. Lola slowly pulled it off, hoping her dirty blond hair would cover her ears. Gunther kept considering her, looking at one side of her face, then the other. She tapped her foot, hoping it would end soon. Whenever someone looked at her that long it only meant one thing: They were forming a joke in their head. "You ahhh eet," he whispered, taking Lola's chin in his hands. "You ahhh my gutta and my light."

Lola blushed so much her ears turned red. She didn't know exactly what that meant, but it sounded good—at least better than needing eye-replacement surgery. "Cheers," Lola said. "I think?"

"You are his Gutter and his Light," Evette explained, exhaling smoke from her cigarette. "It's the name of the new campaign?" She shot Lola a look that said, *Do you have* any *clue why you're here?*

"Yes!" Gunther yelped, stomping a python-skin boot on the floor. "I was in ze gutta! Zen I saw ze light!" He reached his hand up to the ceiling and stared at it for a good minute, his eyes rolling back in his head. Lola looked up, but all she saw was an air-conditioning vent. "Evette!" Gunther yelled, even though Evette was only five feet away from him. "Tell ze ahthas to leeve. I have found her!"

Evette stepped outside and Gunther kept circling Lola like she was a rare species of exotic bird. "You ahh so freeesh looking," he hooted, his smile revealing a chipped front tooth. "I am so in ze love with ze ears!" He reached up to give one of Lola's ears a quick tug.

Lola couldn't stand it any longer. She bounced up and down on her heels, clapping her hands in excitement. *Gunther Gunta* loved her ears. *Gunther Gunta* thought *she* was freeesh looking. She didn't need a lip reduction, an ear tuck, or hair-replacement surgery. And if Gunther Gunta, one of the toughest critics loved her, everyone would.

Gunther grabbed two small cups of green liquid off the credenza and downed them one after the other. Lola recognized the smell as wheatgrass, the organic sludge her mum drank when she was trying to be healthy.

Evette returned and handed Lola a clipboard that had all the details of the shoot. At four o'clock on Saturday she'd show up at a warehouse on Canal Street. Evette pointed to the fine print at the bottom of the contract. "Just two things: You need a guardian to sign, and you cannot, under any circumstances, bathe until then."

"No bathing?" Lola asked. It seemed like an odd request. Her mum had been a model for over twenty years, and she'd never mentioned anything about not showering.

"No baaathing!" Gunther screeched, pounding his little fist in the air. "You aah too be au naturale, one with ze guttaaa." Lola could smell the wheatgrass on his breath, like he'd just eaten a whole bag of lawn clippings. "I had ze girls, zey come in wit ze spritz spritz in ze hair, and zey smeell like ze parfum. Zey put ze powda under their arms, ze powda." He pulled his glasses down his nose and gave her a stern look. "I was in ze guttaaa, Lola. Do you know wut zat meens?"

"No," Lola mumbled, shaking her head.

"Eet meens I wuz in ze feelth. I wuz gnawing on ze old loaf of bread like a dirty leetle rat. So no baaaathing!" He pounded his little fist in the air. "No spritz spritz! No powda or parfum! Understend?"

"Abso-bloody-lutely." Lola nodded. The shoot was only two days away. She didn't have to bathe or use hair spray or perfume. She would roll around in a Dumpster if Gunther Gunta asked her to. He was her boss now, and she was his Gutter and his Light. The little man threw his arms around her one last time before pushing her out the door.

"Saturdaaaay!" he called over her shoulder. "Saturdaaay!"

FROM THE DESK OF CATE SLOANE

Interview questions for Chi Sigma rush

- Have you ever been associated outside of school with Blythe Finley? If so, in what capacity?

- If you could only wear one designer for the rest of your life, who would it be? Please elaborate.

- Barneys is on fire, and your best friend has been trampled by women trying to get out with their sale items. She's badly hurt and can't walk. Do you leave her and go for help, or stay until help arrives? Explain your answer.

- Have you ever been to a Disney show on ice? Have you ever suggested your friends go to a Disney show on ice? If so, please specify dates and which ones.

- You overhear a girl calling a member of your sorority "stuck-up." Do you
    a) immediately confront the girl;
    b) return to your friends and tell them what happened;
    c) convince yourself it didn't happen—that you must've heard wrong; or
    d) pretend you're really mad, but then wave to the girl in gym when your sorority sisters aren't looking.

  Explain your answer.

- Tell us your greatest weakness.

SELECTIVENESS IS NEXT TO GODLINESS

Thursday after school, Cate and Stella sat behind a long oak table in the Ashton Prep drawing room, a wood-paneled hall that smelled faintly of Pledge. A few candidates were lounging on the grand piano in the corner, like they were about to break into show tunes. As more girls trickled in, Cate thumbed through her red Moleskine notebook, wanting to seem poised and professional. She and Stella had stayed up late the night before, writing interview questions and deciding how to seem both intimidating and accessible. Cate had borrowed a gavel from the debate team, and Stella had stolen Margot's red Kate Spade reading glasses.

Cate scanned the room, which was now packed with more than forty girls. Stella had prepared her for a few inevitable disappointments—the flyers had been plastered all over the high school for everyone to see. Liza Bartuzzo and the marching band girls had shown up after all. And Kimberly Berth, the only member of the Ashton mascot club, dragged a purple duffel bag in behind her. But with those few exceptions, the view was pretty good.

Eleanor Donner was there, her black hair falling to her shoulders in shiny barrel curls. Shelley DeWitt had worn a strapless metallic cocktail dress that made her pale skin look radiant. Even Paige Mortimer—a former member of the Chi Beta Phi blacklist—had gone all out, her brown hair swept to the side in a dramatic updo. Cate turned the sapphire ring on her finger, thinking of the time her mother had taken her to FAO Schwarz when she was a little girl. She'd spent two hours wandering the aisles, trying to pick out the perfect porcelain doll. The only difference was, those dolls came perfect. The girls in front of her needed a few *adjustments* to make them Chi Sigma–worthy. Still, it was a solid turnout.

She spotted a familiar face in the back of the room. Andie was standing behind Kimberly Berth, trying to seem inconspicuous. Cate narrowed her blue eyes at Andie. Last year she had discovered Andie and Cindy hiding in her closet during a Chi Beta Phi sleepover, eavesdropping on plans for their weekend trip to the Hamptons. It had always been that way: If Cate bought gray suede Sigerson Morrison boots, the next day Andie was wearing the same ones in black, insisting it was a coincidence. And when Cate got a body wave at Frédéric Fekkai, Andie started wearing her hair wavy too. She'd thought Andie's days of doing bad Cate Sloane impressions were over, but apparently she was wrong. Maybe imitation *was* a form of flattery. But when your little sister was doing the imitating, it felt more like a form of torture.

Cate banged the gavel hard on the wood table and all the girls in the drawing room jumped. "Thank you all for coming," she said, sounding anything but thankful.

"We hope you are all prepared to tell us why you should be the third member of Chi Sigma," Stella said. "If you've brought a CV, we'll take those now. The rest of you can line up."

Paige Mortimer set a black leather folder down in front of Cate and Stella. "Everything is in here." She tapped it gently. "My résumé, my certificate from Junior Honor Society, my headshot from when I was a child actor along with a DVD of the Welch's commercial I was in, three recommendations from Ashton jun—"

"Your older sister doesn't count," Cate interrupted. It was impossible to rely on Paige Mortimer, who was infamous for being two-faced. She changed faster than a braless sixth-grader during gym. Last spring she'd called Cate "stuck-up."

"*Two* recommendations from Ashton juniors," Paige corrected, pulling a piece of paper from the folder and crumpling it up.

Stella looked over the CV. Technically Paige had all the right credentials. But the last thing Chi Sigma needed was someone who'd insist they wear matching J. Crew flowered button-downs every Friday, or argue with Cate over which subway they should take to Columbus Circle. They needed a follower—someone who would be happy doing whatever she and Cate decided. And according to Paige's résumé (*captain of the Ashton Middle School swim team, editor in chief of the middle school newspaper*), she was used to being in the spotlight.

"Now"—Stella tried banging the gavel, just for fun—"we

appreciate you all coming, but we have very specific criteria to follow." She pulled Margot's glasses down to the tip of her nose. The prescription was so strong they made the drawing room look like a Monet painting—everything blurred together.

"Yes," Cate continued, glancing down at her notebook as if it contained important information. "We cannot, under any circumstances, consider any middle school girls." Andie crossed her arms over her chest, obviously annoyed. "Sorry, C.C." Andie left, followed by a girl with an unfortunate mole, and two fifth-graders who were so tiny they looked like they belonged in day care.

"And I'm sorry," Stella added, "but we can't have any candidates affiliated with the Ashton Prep marching band, or the Ashton Prep mascot club." Liza Bartuzzo & Co. slowly collected their flags and headed out, but not before Liza muttered something under her breath that sounded like "discrimination lawsuit." Kimberly "Kimmy-Kim" Berth exited too, dragging her purple duffel bag behind her. The tail of the bobcat costume was sticking out the back, like she'd just bagged game on a hunting safari.

Stella looked down at the list of questions, searching for the perfect opener.

"What is *Mug the Slug* doing here?" Cate hissed in her ear. Stella's head snapped back like a Pez dispenser. Myra Granberry had snuck in the side door, filing in line next to Paige Mortimer. Her thin blond hair was smoothed back into a ponytail, and she had changed into a purple button-down shirt.

"It is an *open* call," Stella whispered, suddenly nervous. She'd completed her biology lab with Myra this morning, labeling all the different chambers of the heart on a worksheet. Myra had talked about her Mathletes practice, the ABC special she'd seen on insomnia in mice, and her dad's prototype for the underwater guitar, but she hadn't mentioned anything about the Chi Sigma rush. Stella was hoping she'd forgotten.

"Sorry I'm late!" Myra said cheerfully, offering Stella a small wave. Myra pulled up her red and white–striped knee-highs, smiling.

Stella cringed. There was no way she was telling her to leave—not now. But if it wasn't for her, Myra would've never showed up in the first place. "So let's begin." Stella adjusted the glasses. "Why do—"

"Wait." Cate interrupted, a smirk creeping across her face. She leveled her deep blue eyes at Myra. "I'm sorry, but we can't accept any candidates with facial hair." Paige Mortimer laughed loudly. Myra glanced from Cate to Stella, tears welling in her eyes.

"She didn't—" Stella tried to find the right words. But before she could say anything else, Myra covered her lip with her hand and stormed out.

"Cate," Stella hissed under the chorus of giggles. "You didn't have to be so harsh."

"Since when are you friends with the Slug?" Cate brushed her dark brown hair out of her eyes, shooting Stella her most innocent *Was it something I said?* look.

"She's my lab partner," Stella snapped. She knew lab partner didn't equal best friend, but suddenly she couldn't stand thinking about Myra sitting alone in the loo, dabbing her eyes with cheap squares of toilet paper. "I'll be right back." Stella darted outside, feeling Cate's stare burning a hole through her back.

"Myra!" she called. "Myra!" The hall was empty except for a few creepy papier-mâché sculptures. The short, abstract blobs looked vaguely like headless children.

"Myra?" a familiar voice asked. Stella whipped around to see Blythe and the Beta Sigma Phis turning the corner. They were in matching red Juicy Couture pants and their hair was pulled back into sweaty ponytails.

"Have you seen her?" Stella asked, peeking into the photography room. Molly Lambert, Ashton's only goth, was hanging framed pictures of a boy in a long black trench coat. "She was just at the open call."

"Are you kidding?" Blythe put a hand on her hip and stuck out her boobs, which she did whenever she felt threatened, the way porcupines shot quills or skunks sprayed that foul musk. "You think *Mug the Slug* is Chi Sigma material?"

"Why not?" Stella asked, already knowing the answer to the question. There were unspoken rules in high school. You didn't wear red and white–striped socks, you didn't talk loudly about your pet ferret, and you definitely didn't walk around with a thick white mustache.

"Oh, come on." Priya tilted her head so that her nose ring caught the light. "Yesterday I heard her telling Mrs. Perkins about her sea monkeys. She's bizarre."

"Well, *I* like her." Stella rested her hands on the top of her gray uniform skirt. It wasn't like Myra was hopeless. She just needed some . . . *guidance.* Instead of shopping with her inventor dad, picking out weird socks and ugly patterned sweaters, she needed go to somewhere like Bloomingdale's, or Saks. "With a few adjustments she *could be* Chi Sigma material."

"I'll believe it when I see it." Blythe laughed.

Stella narrowed her eyes. That sounded like a challenge, and Stella *never* backed down from a challenge. When Robin Lawrence told her she was too young to have a painting in a gallery in London, she'd spent two weeks dragging her abstract self-portrait around Chelsea, until she found a small place that would exhibit it in their "Emerging Artists" show.

"Just watch." Stella smiled. "I'll turn Myra Granberry into one of the most popular girls at Ashton." With that, she turned on her heel, her blond curls bouncing as she strode back into the drawing room. She would use a little green shadow to bring out Myra's brown eyes, and her mustache would come right off with a good threading. They'd find the perfect Cynthia Rowley dress for her petite frame. The makeover would be easy.

Convincing Cate to let Myra be the Mu to their Chi Sigma? *That* would be the hard part.

ELI PUNCH IS HAVERFORD'S BEST CATCH

After the open call, Cate sat in the packed Haverford gymnasium. The fans were all holding red-and-blue pom-poms or flags, like they'd just looted the school store. The Haverford Devil, a twiggy boy dressed in a skintight red bodysuit, aimed something that looked like a grenade launcher at the crowd. A whole row of sixth-grade boys pounded their fists in the air, their faces painted bright red. "Over here!" one called, opening his hands. "Me!"

A woman in tortoiseshell Gucci glasses sat in front of Cate, looking on in disapproval. She grabbed her husband's arm. "I don't know whose idea it was to get him that T-shirt cannon. He's going to kill someone." As the players made their way down the court, the Devil shot a balled-up shirt into the bleachers. It careened over the boys' heads, hitting a white-haired man squarely in the chest. He held up the blue Haverford Basketball T-shirt and the crowd cheered. "I should call the dean," the woman continued. "Really." Cate wished Stella was there, but

Ashton's headmistress had called her into a lame *How are you adjusting?* meeting after the rush. She needed someone to roll her eyes with—someone to sit beside her when Eli glanced up into the stands.

She imagined wearing a Haverford Basketball T-shirt next weekend, when she was helping Eli unpack his room. He'd pull her close and kiss her forehead, a thank-you for supporting his team. "I don't know." Cate leaned forward, interrupting their conversation. "It could be kind of . . . *fun.*" The woman shook her head, like Cate had just told her she supported school-sponsored bungee jumping.

On the court below, Eli chest-passed to Braden Pennyworth, his arms glistening with sweat. Cate smiled. She'd worn her dark wash J Brand jeans and bright red Madison Marcus silk top, which she hoped would send a clear message to Eli: *I am enthusiastic about your athletic pursuits, but I am also fashion forward.* She'd only been to one Haverford basketball game before, when she was twelve, and that was because her dad had dragged her. While she loved being part of the Ashton drama club, or heading the fall formal committee, she'd always thought sports functions weren't for her. But as she watched Eli dribble up the court, his toned arms flexed and his black hair an adorable sweaty mop, she knew she'd been wrong. At the very least, she could enjoy the view.

Eli did a layup and the ball swished through the net. As he high-fived his teammates, the stands erupted in cheers. The boys with the red faces chest-bumped each other and the Devil shook his skinny butt at the crowd, his pointed tail swinging back and forth. "Yes!" Cate shrieked. She waved her Haverford flag so fast she nearly poked the Botoxed mother next to her in the eye. "Go Eli! Yes!"

When she sat down, the woman was staring at her. Her skin was completely smooth, like she hadn't made a facial expression in years. "That's my next-door neighbor," Cate explained. She couldn't wait for the moment when she could officially call Eli her boyfriend. It was only a matter of time. Earlier today Danny had overheard him mentioning a "cute freshman from Ashton Prep." It was practically a done deal.

The clock counted down the last second of the first half and the team exchanged pats on the back. Eli walked off the court and took a swig from his water bottle. His eyes scanned the stands.

"He's looking for you," the woman whispered, pointing a manicured nail at Eli. Cate felt like her whole body was on fire. Every moment she'd thought about him, pored over the "Green Club" folder, memorizing his schedule, or Google Earthing his address in Westport, was now worth it. Because every moment she'd been thinking about Eli, *Eli* had been thinking about *her*.

Cate watched Eli's brown eyes searching the sea of faces. *I'm over here,* she thought. She sat up straighter and pursed some color into her lips. *Over here.* The Haverford Devil had picked up the T-shirt cannon and was aiming it at the stands again. He pulled the trigger, sending a red ball flying in Cate's direction. She saw her opportunity and stood up, feeling Eli watching her from the court below. The T-shirt sailed closer and she reached up, ready to grab it as it flew by.

"I've got it!" she cried. All the people around her, even the woman with the tortoise glasses, cheered as it came closer. She stood on her tippytoes, as it came closer still, but it flew right between her hands.

"No—*I've* got it," a voice said. Cate whipped around. Blythe, overly tanned Boobie Blythe, was in the stands a few rows back. Sophie and Priya were next to her, and they were all a mess of Haverford paraphernalia. Not only were they wearing Haverford warm-ups, they had every accessory you could possibly buy— pom-poms, foam fingers, and flags. Blythe was wearing devil horns, which suited her perfectly. "Eli!" she yelled, holding the T-shirt up. "Look!"

Cate turned back to the court where Eli was standing, smiling and waving at Blythe. She dug her nails into her palm. That smile. It was so genuine, so adorable, and so *not* directed at her.

Blythe blew a kiss to him. "Isn't he the best?" she asked, leveling her eyes at Cate. "We have a date tomorrow." She leaned to her right, trying to look around Cate. "Do you mind? You're blocking my view."

Cate clenched her fists tight. Blythe had a date with *her* next-door neighbor, *her* crush, *her* future boyfriend. She already had Priya and Sophie. Now she was taking Eli Punch too?

LITTLE WHITE LIES ARE THE WORST KIND

Thursday afternoon Andie sat at her desk, her hands trembling with excitement. For the third day in a row she was talking to Kyle Lewis on IM. It turned out Kyle went snowboarding every winter at Killington too, and they were both obsessed with the New England clam chowder they served at the lodge. They both agreed that *Sam's Town* was the Killers' worst album, with the exception of "Read My Mind"—which was by far the best song they'd ever written. They even went to the same soccer camp in New Hampshire last summer, just on different weeks. It was starting to feel like Kyle was the boy version of herself.

STRIKER15: WHAT R U UP 2 2MORROW?
SLOANE28: NM. Y?
STRIKER15: U SHOULD COME 2 MY BAND PRACTICE
STRIKER15: WE REHEARSE AT THE LIVING ROOM
STRIKER15: U CAN HEAR ALL OUR NEW SONGS
SLOANE28: SOUNDS AMAZING

Andie's legs felt like they were made of oatmeal. The Living Room was a music hall on the Lower East Side that Andie had only read about in *New York* magazine. She pictured her and Kyle sitting at a table after the practice ended and his band had gone home. He'd lean over her shoulder, his hand on top of hers, showing her how to play a G chord. They'd walk around the neighborhood, stopping at Sugar Sweet Sunshine for the peanut butter pie Andie was obsessed with. It would be their first official date.

"Andie!" Lola's voice echoed off the bathroom walls.

SLOANE28: G2G

Andie slammed the laptop shut, feeling like she'd just been caught stealing from Cate's closet. There was still one problem with her date with Kyle: Lola. But even if they *had* gone on a date to Madame Tussauds, even if Lola *had* "fancied" him, she hadn't mentioned anything about it since the fight on Saturday—not a word. Andie was starting to think she'd forgotten about the whole thing. After all, if Andie were the one meeting Gunther Gunta and his entourage of French socialites, or swapping calls with Ayana Bennington, she definitely wouldn't be obsessing over her childhood best friend.

"You were right!" Lola cried, bursting into Andie's room. She was still wearing her black chiffon dress and the shimmery white MAC eye shadow Andie had managed to apply two hours ago, even though Lola flinched whenever the brush came within an inch of her eye. "Gunther loved me! I'm heeezzz guttaaa and light." Lola clapped her hands in front of her face as she impersonated Gunther's accent.

"Wow." Andie tried hard to smile, but her cheeks were numb, like she'd just gotten a cavity drilled. She'd been prepared for Lola to meet Gunther, but she wasn't prepared for Gunther to make Lola the next Kate Moss. Most models spent years doing minor advertising campaigns, switching agents, and even then few ever went on a go-see with someone as renowned as Gunther Gunta. Lola's modeling career had gone from zero to sixty in less than a week, while Andie's was in the same place it had always been: nowhere.

"Congratulations." Andie wrapped her stepsister in a hug, her arms feeling like Jell-O. "I can't believe you're going to work for Gunther Gunta." She took a deep breath, trying to steady her voice. Talking to Kyle was officially the only good thing that had happened all day. After Cate threw her out of the Chi Sigma open call, she was so mad, she'd picked two of Cate's favorite dresses out of her closet and hid them under her dresser. Then she'd written *Cate was here* on the top of her dad's rolltop desk with a ballpoint pen, so he would find it when he got back from the honeymoon. Sometimes she just wanted him to see that Cate wasn't perfect. Maybe she had better grades than Andie, maybe she was the lead in the play and the president of Junior Honor Society, but she had more sides than an octagon. And she could be cruel—even to her own sister.

"Oh, he's a complete nutter!" Lola continued. She threw herself on Andie's queen-size bed and rolled onto her stomach, scattering the red and orange–embroidered throw pillows in every direction. "He kept on about me not 'baaaathing,' and how 'freeesh' looking I am. And he's even shorter than you!"

Andie sat back on the bed, a little stung. She knew Lola didn't mean anything by calling her short. It was just a fact. Andie was four foot ten and three quarters, and Lola was five seven and a half. But still, Andie didn't need any reminders.

Lola squeezed the throw pillow in her hand. "And this is going to change everything with Kyle."

"Kyle?" Andie grabbed a fistful of blankets in her hand. His name suddenly sounded strange coming out of Lola's mouth. It was as if Andie had caught Lola wearing her favorite pair of J Brand jeans, or telling people *she* played soccer.

"Once he sees me in those ads, with my hair done and wearing a Gunther Gunta dress, he'll really fancy me." Lola stared out the window, as if picturing Kyle looking up at her billboard in Times Square. "I've barely talked to him since Saturday, though. Every time I ask him to hang out he's doing homework, or going to dinner with his parents. I asked him if I could go to his band practice on Friday, but he said I'd probably be bored."

"Really?" Andie squeaked. She reached for her ponytail, but all her movements felt slow and forced. There was her answer. Lola *was* still interested in Kyle.

Lola pulled a bright yellow throw pillow to her chest. "I don't know what I did. Everything was brilliant until Saturday. I know I shouldn't have pushed him out of the door, but still."

"You probably didn't do anything." Andie's palms were slick with sweat. The room felt hot, the way it had last August when the central air was broken for two days. "Why don't we go get Pinkberry?" she offered, trying to change the subject.

Lola ignored her, her green eyes focused on a spot on the ceiling. "It's like he has a girlfriend or something." The end of her freckled nose twitched. "Do you think I should ask him about it?"

"No!" Andie snapped. She pulled at the collar of her mint green Lacoste button-down, feeling like it was choking her. "Definitely not. Just . . . give him some time."

Lola narrowed her green eyes at her stepsister. "You're acting barmy." She'd never seen Andie so nervous before, even when they went to Ford Models to meet Ayana. Her cheeks were bright red and she kept staring at her patent leather flats. Lola had seen a special on the BBC once, on how investigators determine if someone is lying. Avoiding eye contact was the number-two way, right under stiff body movements. Lola looked past Andie, where a boy's gray hoodie was slung over the end of the bed. She eyed it, suddenly suspicious. It looked just like the one Kyle had worn to Madame Tussauds. "Why do you have that boy's sweatshirt in your room? Whose is that?"

"This?" Andie held up the sweatshirt. She'd completely forgotten about Kyle's hoodie. She'd been holding on to it since Tuesday, wearing it every now and then before she went to bed. She looked at Lola, her heart pounding like she'd just run ten sprints, one after the next, after the next. "This is . . ." She searched her brain, trying to think of something—anything. She couldn't tell Lola about Kyle now, not after it was so completely obvious she was still obsessed with him. "This is . . . *Clay Calhoun's*."

"Clay Calhoun?" Lola furrowed her brows. "Why do you have *Clay Calhoun's* sweatshirt?" She'd only been at Ashton Prep a week and a half, but she'd learned who Clay Calhoun was before she learned her homeroom. All the Ashton girls kept on about him like he was Prince Harry or something.

"He's," Andie heard herself say, "my new boyfriend." She shot Lola a smile that said, *Isn't that just so crazy?* So it wasn't the truth. It wasn't even a small sliver of the truth. But how could she have possibly explained the shirt?

"You're dating *Clay Calhoun*?" Lola asked, clapping her hands in front of her face. "Since when?"

"Since Tuesday," Andie hugged the sweatshirt to her chest. "I just didn't want to say anything . . ." One lie came after the other, tumbling out of her mouth. She couldn't stop them now.

"I can't believe you didn't tell me." Lola threw her pale arms around Andie. "And here I was keeping on about Gunther Gunta. This is brilliant."

As Lola squeezed all the air out of her lungs, Andie stared at the digital picture frame on her desk. It was on a photo of her and Lola at the wedding. They were holding their bridesmaid bouquets, their arms wrapped around one another like they had known each other forever. Her stomach sank with guilt.

"I can't wait to meet him," Lola said. "I heard he's the fittest bloke at Haverford."

"Yeah . . . he's great," Andie lied. Technically, Clay *was* "the fittest bloke at Haverford." And he was an expert at making armpit farts, butt buddies with Brandon O'Rourke, and the son of Scooter Calhoun, who'd somehow managed to become the CEO of a major investment bank despite his name. Clay Calhoun was a lot of things. But he wasn't Andie's boyfriend. Not even close.

THE LIFE OF THE PARTY IS . . .
MYRA GRANBERRY?

Stella and Cate sat at the round cherry table in the kitchen, staring at the list of candidates from the open call. Margot was pulling things out of the refrigerator. Her hair was in curlers and she was humming to herself like some lovesick princess in a Disney movie.

"Lindsey Krauss?" Stella read from the Moleskine notebook in front of her.

"Who?" Cate set her head down on the table. She couldn't muster any enthusiasm for Chi Sigma, not after her run-in with Blythe at the basketball game. They were in a serious clique war, and right now all she wanted to do was fly the white flag of surrender. Blythe had Priya, Sophie, *and* Eli Punch. On all sides, she was winning.

"Well, I guess that's our answer. She's quiet, just transferred from public school. Kind of looks like she got hit in the face with a frying pan?" Stella raised her eyebrows as if to say, *Does any of this ring a bell?*

"She's obviously forgettable." Cate doodled on the spiral note-book in front of her. She drew a crude picture of Blythe, complete with devil horns and fangs. All she needed was an orange crayon to color in her skin.

Margot dumped a whole avocado, milk, and some honey into the blender. "Hope I'm not bothering you!" she yelled over the electronic mixing sound. "I'm just making my secret anti-aging masque! I've been using it since the '80s!"

"It's fine, Grandmum." Stella pressed her fingers to her temples until the blender stopped. Margot had gone to "Capri" for three weeks last year and come back with flawless skin that was three shades lighter than her neck. Still, she insisted she owed every-thing to that avocado sludge.

"Yes, Lindsey is too forgettable," Stella continued. "We both say nay. But we also don't want someone who needs to be the center of attention." She studied Cate's face, giving the words a moment to sink in. She hadn't brought up Myra's makeover yet. First she wanted to show Cate that all of the other candidates were inadequate—a task that seemed easier and easier with each name she read off. There'd been more nays than on the horse path through Central Park. Cate hadn't even given an official "nay" to Shelley DeWitt, but had simply writhed in pain, like someone was poking her with a hot iron. "That said, I don't think Paige Mortimer is a good candidate. I say nay."

"Me neither. Nay!" Cate grabbed the notebook from Stella's hand and glanced down the list. "Last year Corynne Handler spread a rumor that I had lice, and Marissa Marks chews too loudly." Cate crossed off ten names in a row. "Nay, nay, nay,

nay—I don't like any of these options. This is hopeless. Blythe is going to date Eli, and everyone will always think of Chi Sigma as my lame attempt to start a sorority after she kicked me out of hers."

Cate banged her forehead hard against the table. She imagined going to the winter formal with Stella as her date. They'd hover by the refreshments table, stuffing their faces with Brie and crackers while Blythe slow danced with Eli, her arms wrapped around his neck. She and Stella would sit in English class sophomore year, watching *Ashton News*'s coverage of Blythe's second term as class president. At graduation they'd be forced to listen to Blythe deliver her valedictory address, while Cate was ranked third, the close-but-not-quite spot of every year. *I'd like to thank my best friends, Priya and Sophie,* Blythe would say, *and my loving, supportive boyfriend, Eli Punch.* Her gray eyes would settle on Cate. *I couldn't have done this without you three.*

"It's not *that* awful," Stella said. She chewed the end of her pen. Ever since the basketball game, Cate hadn't stopped talking about Blythe's date with Eli, or how Priya and Sophie had looked at her like she was just another pom-pom-waving basketball mom. Even worse, Cate was still wearing that bloody Tiffany locket under her Lacoste button-down, and the stuffed bear Blythe had bought her was still sitting on her bed. Yes, she'd burned most of her memories of Chi Beta Phi. But Stella was worried she'd forgotten how Chi Beta Phi had burned *her.* If things kept on like this, it wouldn't be long before Cate was begging Blythe to be back in Beta Sigma Phi, pitching a vice president position. Stella would come into school on Monday and be friendless, again, doomed to spend study halls chatting with Mrs. Perkins about her recent vacation to Mohegan Sun.

"You have got to try this," Margot cooed, oblivious to Cate's despair. She mixed the green paste around in a bowl and dabbed some on her face. It looked like someone had sneezed on her.

"Ew, no thanks." Stella winced.

"Suit yourself, but it's great for your complexion. I've got a date this Saturday night and I need to look refreshed." Stella suppressed the urge to roll her eyes. After her grandpa died five years ago, her grandmum had lost her bloody mind. Stella and Lola had spent last summer with her in Florence, watching in horror as she chatted up Italian waiters in the Piazza della Signoria. "It's with Walter Hodgeworth—the retired oil tycoon."

Just yesterday, Stella had seen Walter Hodgeworth on the cover of her grandmum's *Time* magazine, under the headline "The New Rockefeller." Even if he was the most well off bachelor in Manhattan, his white hair receded in an M and his face looked like a shriveled apple.

"Walter's taking me to Masa. I'll need you luvs to keep an eye on Lola and Andie. If everything goes well, I won't be back until late." She winked at Stella before heading out of the kitchen, the green muck concoction in one hand and a dirty martini in the other.

"Repulsive," Cate mumbled under her breath. But Stella was smiling like Margot had just offered to take them to Spain for the weekend. "What?"

"This is *perfect*," Stella whispered. She didn't want to think of her grandmum snogging a walking prune either, but this was the opportunity they needed. "We'll throw a party. We'll invite all the ninth-graders, and you can invite Eli."

Cate suddenly perked up. "Keep talking . . ."

"We'll use it to show Ashton Prep what Chi Sigma is all about. Imagine this." Stella turned to the wall of windows overlooking the garden. She spread her hands in the air dramatically, framing the teak patio furniture. "You're sitting in the garden. It's filled with Ashton girls and Haverford blokes talking about how great Chi Sigma is—how great *Cate Sloane* is. Eli Punch walks in and sees you in your new Kate Spade dress—"

"Nope," Cate corrected, holding one finger in the air. "Kate Spade dresses make me look frumpy."

"Fine—your new Phillip Lim dress—and he completely forgets about Blythe Finley. It's like—*poof!* She doesn't exist." Stella studied Cate's face as she considered it. No one was going to pay any attention to them if they were just eating turkey burgers at Jackson Hole, or walking down Fifth Avenue, mixed in with the other eight million people in New York City. If they wanted to get Chi Sigma off the ground, they needed to make a big statement—regardless of who their third member was. They needed to do something that said, *Here we are. Prepare to worship us.*

"I think"—Cate smiled—"you're a genius."

Stella scrawled *Party* on the top of the page and underlined it with one swift flourish. Just last weekend, she and Cate had planned a small, tasteful wedding in the garden after Winston and Emma called off theirs (which was partially her and Cate's fault, but still). They'd found caterers, a florist, even a band, all in less than twenty-four hours. If the Chi Sigma party was even half as successful, Stella would finally be known at Ashton Prep as more than "the new girl with the funny accent." If everyone came to *their* town house Saturday, for *their* party, she'd be Stella Childs again: the girl who was studying Vermeer before she was ten, the girl who was featured in *Allure* magazine for her fashion designs, the girl whom everyone in school—including the security guards and cafeteria ladies—knew by name. And standing alongside Stella in Chi Sigma, Cate would realize she never needed Blythe to be popular. She needed *Stella*.

"There's still one problem." Cate drummed her manicured nails on the table. "We can't have a party without a third member. It's just embarrassing."

"I was thinking about that . . ." Stella began. "What about Myra Granberry?" She mumbled the name so it came out sounding like "maybe cranberry."

"*Myra Granberry?*" Cate waited for Stella to laugh or say *kidding*. But her green eyes stayed focused on Cate. "The same Myra Granberry that I kicked out of our open call because I couldn't look at her caterpillar lip?" As far as Cate knew, there was only one Mug the Slug. Had Stella lost her mind? "I take that back. You're not a genius. That would be social suicide." They might as well stop shaving their armpits and start wearing sweatpants every day, and simply resign themselves to life as Ashton Prep bottom dwellers. Maybe, if they were lucky, Blythe would let them check coats at their next Beta Sigma Phi soiree.

"Just listen," Stella started, ignoring Cate's outburst. She had already thought of every possible argument against it. "Myra's like a blank canvas. She'll do whatever we say. You never have to worry about her getting jealous or trying to stage a coup. And she's genuinely nice and smart and," Stella added, raising her voice before Cate could object, "all she needs is a very thorough makeover."

"I don't have time for makeovers." Cate ran her hands through her dark brown hair, like she was about to pull it out at the roots. "I have a hot neighbor to stalk."

"Stalk away!" Stella insisted. "I'll do everything for the makeover. In two days I'll turn Myra into the BFF you never knew you needed." Stella looked into Cate's deep blue eyes. Yes, she was pushing this because she'd already promised Blythe a new Myra, but it would be good for Cate too. Cate needed someone who wouldn't argue if she wanted to go all the way to the Lower East Side for Sunday brunch. She needed someone who would not only remember her birthday, but would bake a banana bread "cake" because she knew Cate hated sweets. Myra Granberry was a good choice—the best choice.

Cate shook her head. "I'm not into it."

"Well, that's a shame," Stella started. If *she* couldn't convince Cate, there was one person who could. She hadn't wanted to play this card, but desperate times called for desperate measures. "Because I bumped into Blythe today. She was keeping on about how we could never turn Myra Granberry into sorority material."

"*Blythe* said that?" Cate's face twisted in anger, like someone had poured paint all over her new Antik Batik boots. "What does she know about the capabilities of Chi Sigma?"

"The greatest satisfaction is to do well what Blythe said we could not do at all." Stella leaned forward. "Myra could be our Mu."

"Our Mu," Cate repeated. She imagined Myra strolling down the staircase at the party in a Marc Jacobs dress, her blond hair pulled back in a tight bun. She'd be like some *What Not to Wear* success story, and Chi Sigma would be the ones who'd made it happen. "It *would* be pretty impressive if you could pull it off. If we can transform Mug the Slug into the new Ashton It girl, think of how that would raise our profile."

"Just trust me," Stella added, her pen perched in the air. "I'll make it happen. Saturday, at the party, she'll make her big debut."

Cate twirled her dark brown hair around her finger, considering it. Myra had been an outcast ever since third grade, when her mom sent her to school wearing those awful knee-high socks. It was something Cate never questioned, like grass being green or the sky being blue. But besides the obvious things—her M.U.G. backpack and bleached 'stache—there wasn't anything *that* wrong with Myra. Technically, she was the reason Cate's mock trial team had won last year in Mr. Hertz's social studies class. Knee-highs or no knee-highs, she'd delivered the most persuasive closing arguments Cate had ever heard. "Okay," Cate finally agreed. "I trust you."

Stella scrawled *Myra Granberry* across the top of her notebook, just because it seemed like a satisfying thing to do. She studied her writing, excited. Blythe could go on a date with Eli. She could beg Cate to return to Beta Sigma Phi without Stella. It wouldn't matter. Stella and Cate were finally on the same page, and Blythe couldn't stop them now.

An hour later, Cate paced the living room in her Juicy Couture sweats. "Yes, Dad," she said into her iPhone. "We're being good for Margot." She glanced at Stella and winked. "Right, love you too." With that, she hung up. Winston had called ten minutes ago, as though he could sense they were planning a party, even from Tahiti.

"What did he say?" Stella asked nervously.

"Just that he and your mom went snorkeling today. As long as we have everything cleaned up before Margot gets home, we'll be fine." Cate stood between the chaise lounge and the fireplace. "Now . . . let's see. We can set up the Bose sound dock here; we just need to bring it down from the den." She and Stella had carefully put together a guest list, being more selective than a gluten-free vegan at an all-you-can-eat buffet. They'd even found a bakery online that could make chocolates in the shape of Greek letters. If Chi Sigma Mu's first official soiree was going to establish their dominance, every detail—right down to the customized M&M's—needed to be perfect. "If we have the food in the kitchen, we can keep everyone on the first floor and in the garden."

"Brilliant. Then we can use the den as a VIP area. Every party needs to have a *flow*," Stella agreed. She was wearing her red Topshop shorts, and her curls were pulled back in a ponytail.

"Party?" a voice asked. Cate turned to see Lola and Andie hovering in the doorway, both chewing on chocolate granola bars. Lola clapped her hands small and fast in front of her face, more hyper than a fifth-grader with ADD.

"Isn't it past your bedtime?" Cate leaned on the white marble mantel. She eyed Lola's pajamas, which were patterned with Hogwarts crests.

"When are you throwing a party?" Lola asked, ignoring Cate's question. Even if Kyle hadn't been the greatest friend all week, a party would be a brilliant excuse to invite him to the town house.

"It's Saturday," Cate said.

Lola clapped her hands together excitedly. Saturday was the day of her Gunther Gunta shoot! She'd walk into the town house after the shoot, her hair slicked back, her face made up, wearing a couture evening gown. It would be the perfect time for Kyle to meet the new, improved Lola Childs—the supermodel.

"But it's an upper-school party," Cate continued. "So run along now." She made a shooing gesture with her hand, like the one Emma used when Heath Bar was digging his claws into the furniture. Lola slumped against the doorway, disappointed.

"Sorry." Stella shrugged.

Andie took a bite of granola bar and swallowed hard. She hadn't seen Cate since she humiliated her at the Chi Sigma open call. Sometimes it was hard to believe this was the same person who'd read her *The Very Hungry Caterpillar* in their mother's library, making up any words she didn't recognize. If Cate didn't want to be her friend, fine. They would never be friends. But Andie wasn't going to be treated like a boarder in her own house. "Does Margot know about this?" she challenged.

"Margot won't care." Cate grabbed a notebook off the mantel and started scribbling in it.

Andie squeezed the granola bar in her hand, nearly shooting it out of the wrapper. That was how Cate always ended their conversations—by starting something else.

"Then maybe I'll just go tell her," she said. She turned on her heel, her glossy ponytail swishing back and forth. She got through the foyer and up the first two stairs before she heard Cate's voice over her shoulder.

"Fine!" she called. "You can come."

Andie slunk back to the doorway, feeling more satisfied than when she scored on Tricia Kipps, the obnoxious Donalty goalie who was always trash-talking before games. "*And* we can invite friends," she negotiated.

"You're pushing it," Cate huffed. Her pale cheeks were splotchy and red, the way they always got when she was angry.

"Margot!" Andie yelled up the stairs.

But before she could say anything else, Cate cut her off. "Fine—no losers, though."

Andie took off into the foyer, feeling a sudden burst of energy.

"You're brilliant!" Lola cried. She darted up the stairs, pulling Andie by the hand. "Now you can invite Clay. I can't wait to meet him."

Andie's entire body slowed, her feet feeling like they were made of lead. Three hours had passed since her little white lie, and she wasn't any closer to having Clay Calhoun as her boyfriend. She needed a plan—and fast.

TO: Clay Calhoun
FROM: Andie Sloane
DATE: Thursday, 10:05 p.m.
SUBJECT: Hey . . .

Hey there,
I forgot to tell you how great you were at the
scrimmage on Tuesday. That goal you scored came
out of nowhere. I was telling my friend Kyle, you're
the best one on the Haverford team. Way better than
Austin Thorpe.
Are you still around tomorrow? We should
definitely hang out.

xoxo
Andie

TO: Andie Sloane
FROM: Clay Calhoun
DATE: Thursday, 10:28 p.m.
SUBJECT: Re: Hey . . .

Hey Sloane,

I was wondering what the deal was with that toolbag. He goes to Donalty, right? Austin hates that kid.

Yeah, I'm around tomorrow. We should hang out. Brandon and I are playing Ultimate Frisbee on the Great Lawn anyway, so I can come by your house around 4:30.

Clay

GOODBYE MUG THE SLUG, HELLO MYRA GRANBERRY

"Myra!" Stella pounded on the wood door. "Please—open up!"

"I told you," a voice echoed from inside the bathroom. "I don't want to see your face!" It was Friday afternoon, and the school was practically empty. But Stella was standing outside the eighth-floor loo, waiting for Myra to emerge. Since the open call, Myra hadn't responded to any of her e-mails. She'd tried everything: explaining (*I followed you out but I couldn't find you*), pretending it didn't happen (*Are you free for lunch tomorrow?*), and finally defending (*It's not my fault Cate said that*). Then this morning, in biology, Myra had moved her seat to a table in the corner, telling Mrs. Perkins she preferred to learn about mitosis alone. Stella had been so busy convincing Blythe and Cate that she could turn Myra into Chi Sigma material, she hadn't run the idea by Myra herself.

Stella glanced at the clock on the wall. It was four sixteen. Which meant Myra had been barricaded in the loo for twelve minutes, ever since Stella followed her there after her Mathlete practice. She had to come out eventually, at least for food. And when she did, Stella would plead her case, tell her how the facial hair comment was just Cate's way of expressing affection (*She loves to tease!*) and Chi Sigma would be delighted to have her as its third member. Myra would understand it had all been one horrid misunderstanding.

Or not.

The door swung open, nearly knocking Stella in the face. "Stay away from me!" Myra growled, storming down the hallway. A portrait of Lady Harriet Ashton hung on the far wall. She watched the scene unfold, her lips pursed in disappointment.

Stella managed to grab Myra's arm, but she flailed about wildly, trying to break free. Missy Hurst, a junior Stella recognized from art class, was sitting on a leather couch in the lounge. She glanced at the bright red emergency phone on the wall, not sure what to do. "Bloody hell, Myra!" Stella cried. "It wasn't my fault!"

Hearing those words, Myra froze and pointed a finger in Stella's face. "Wasn't your fault? *You're* the one who told me to show up. *You* said I had a good chance!" Her brown eyes were wet. Under her white button-down she was wearing an EASY AS π T-shirt, the writing just barely visible. "Did you enjoy watching everyone laugh at me?"

Stella remembered Myra's face in the drawing room, how she'd gone ashen when Cate mentioned her facial hair. "No. . . ." Her stomach felt queasy, like she might puke her brown rice sushi all over the floor. "I just didn't think—"

"No." Myra cut her off. "You didn't think." With that, she stalked off down the hall.

Stella watched her go, the monogrammed L.L. Bean backpack bouncing high on her shoulders. With the exception of her mum, no one ever talked to Stella that way. Not Pippa. Not Bridget. Not even Lola, during their most horrid fights. But technically, it *was* her fault. She knew how Cate would react, and she'd told Myra to come anyway. Stella recognized something unexpected in Myra's words, something she hadn't even realized she'd been missing: the truth.

"Wait!" Stella called. She wrung her hands together, searching for the right thing to say. "I'm sorry." Myra froze. "I'm really sorry." She turned around and looked Stella in the eyes, her face softer than before. "We want you as our third member," Stella continued. "We're having our first sorority party tomorrow night, and we want you there, as our Mu."

"What?" Myra's forehead wrinkled in confusion, like Stella had just told her E did not equal MC squared. "What do you mean?"

"Chi Sigma . . . Mu. We reviewed the candidates. We want you." Stella walked down the hall toward her. "And Cate is . . . sorry."

"*Cate Sloane* said she's sorry for making fun of me? Somehow I don't believe that." Myra crossed her arms over her chest.

Stella leaned in close, so only Myra could hear. "Look, we're not letting Paige Mortimer in, or Corynne Handler—they've been trying to tear Cate down for the last three years." Stella was being honest. Myra would never spread lies about Cate having lice, call her stuck up, or threaten to tell the entire school about Stella's dad and Cloud McClean. Myra was someone they could trust.

"This isn't some kind of joke, is it?" Myra studied Stella's face.

Stella thought about Blythe's challenge, how she'd insisted she could make Myra Chi Sigma material. It wasn't a joke. The bet was more of an . . . *inspiration* . . . than anything else. Still, it was better if Myra didn't know about it. "Not at all," Stella said. She threaded her arm through Myra's and they walked down the hall together. "What do you think? Are you in?"

Myra nodded slowly. "I'm in."

"Good," Stella said, her lips curling into a smile. "Now there's just one thing we need to do before the party tomorrow. . . ."

Stella sat under the colander-looking dryer, the air whooshing around her foiled head. Every seat in the Red Door Salon was filled. A wrinkled old lady was getting the yellowed soles of her feet pumiced while a Botoxed man in a navy Christian Dior turtleneck examined his clear polish manicure. Stella glanced nervously at her dainty Movado watch. "Excuse me," she asked, waving at a stylist with a trendy, twentieth-century version of the mullet. Even now, it was still ugly. "Did you see where my friend Myra went? White-blond hair? EASY AS π T-shirt?" The stylist shook her head.

After school, Stella had taken Myra to the Elizabeth Arden salon. The threading artist had disappeared with Myra almost an hour ago. Stella cringed as she imagined Myra in one of the back rooms, squirming in pain as a team held her down and threaded off all her arm hair. Myra would emerge tiny, shiny, and pink, like a newborn hairless Chihuahua.

A woman peeked out from behind a door that said MAKEUP. She had a pure white tuft of hair in her black bangs, like Pepé Le Pew. "Your friend . . . is ready," she said. Stella set her *Vogue* down in her lap, suddenly nervous.

Pepé opened the door and out stepped Myra's beautiful cousin. Her thin blond hair was cut into a chic Katie Holmes bob, showing off her high cheekbones and plump, heart-shaped lips. Her deep-set amber eyes shone beneath her brows, which were suddenly visible after being filled out with light brown pencil. Her face was still pink from the threading, but it was completely flawless. All her bleached lip fuzz was gone.

Stella stood up, knocking her head on the plastic dome. Myra was still Myra, with her rainbow knee-high socks and her EASY AS π T-shirt, but she looked . . . different. She looked . . . incredible. "You're bloody gorgeous!" Stella cried.

Myra smiled shyly, her glossy lips catching the light. She spotted her reflection in the mirror on the wall and spun around once, touching the bottom of her bob. "I like it—I really like it."

Stella had never seen Myra like this before. She wasn't hunched over, staring at her Vans the way she always did when she walked around Ashton Prep. Her shoulders were back, making her look at least three inches taller. And she couldn't stop smiling. "When you walk into the party tomorrow, those Haverford blokes are going to keel over."

Myra kept looking at her reflection, moving closer and closer to the mirror, the way Stella did when she was examining her pores. She hadn't heard a word Stella said. "I've never felt so . . . *pretty*," she whispered, her brown eyes wet with tears.

Stella felt something stirring inside her, something that tickled her nose and formed a lump at the back of her throat. She'd planned on giving Myra a new haircut, maybe some new shoes and a gauzy T-shirt that didn't have a math slogan scrawled across the front of it. But she'd done something better—Myra was *happy*. "You were always pretty," she corrected. "You just needed a little help letting it show."

Myra pulled Stella into a tight hug. "Thank you," she said softly, her cheek pressing into Stella's foiled hair. "Thanks."

HAVERFORD INTELLIGENCE FOR CATE SLOANE

REPORTED BY DANNY PLIMPTON:
SEVENTH-GRADER HMS

Wednesday 9:16 a.m.: The Eagle is spotted in the bathroom blowing his nose. The Eagle may have slight cold.

Wednesday 11:49 a.m.: The Eagle tells an unidentified friend that he got lost walking home through Central Park yesterday.

Wednesday 12:30 p.m.: The Eagle discloses to Mrs. Hearth, the Haverford librarian, that *Catcher in the Rye* is his favorite book.

Wednesday 4:42 p.m.: The Eagle spotted at the Museum of Modern Art, staring at a Dalí painting.

Wednesday 6:22 p.m.: The Eagle spotted walking a yellow Labrador retriever on Seventy-seventh Street. He was carrying what looks like a small plastic bag of poop.

Thursday 10:36 a.m.: Three tenth-graders refer to the Eagle as "a cool guy."

Thursday 1:53 p.m.: The Eagle seems to be fully recovered from cold. Has not been seen sneezing or blowing nose for the entire day.

BATTLE OF THE BOYFRIENDS

Kyle leaned so close to the microphone he was practically kissing it. "And you say," he sang, strumming his electric guitar wildly, "It's o-kaay . . . and that's okay with meeee." Behind him the drummer, a stocky boy wearing a Brooklyn Industries hoodie, smashed the cymbals. Kyle's dark brown hair was soaked with sweat, and he kept shaking his head, trying to get it out of his eyes.

"So that's why he wears the aviators and headband!" Andie whispered, digging her fingers into Cindy's arm. They'd gone to the Living Room after school to see the Wormholes practice. Andie had picked out a teal Cynthia Rowley racerback dress and Cindy had changed into her "Lower East Side hipster outfit": a vintage plaid shift dress, brown Sigerson Morrison ankle boots, and a gray fedora with a red feather in it. In sixth grade she'd heard a celebrity stylist say, "Only confident people wear hats," so she'd tried to incorporate one into every ensemble since.

The bright orange room was packed with empty tables. In the

back a man with a green Mohawk swept the floor, getting ready for the night's shows. "And that's okay with meeee," Kyle sang, holding the last note a little longer than the others. He looked out at Andie and smiled, revealing his dimple. She felt the blood rush to her cheeks. She was watching the Wormholes—the same band she and Cindy had listened to on repeat for all of June. They'd sprawled out on her red velvet couch and studied every picture on the band's website, trying to decide which member was the cutest. The decision was unanimous: *K.L.* And now she was dating him.

"Did you see how he just looked at you?" Cindy shrieked. Then she narrowed her eyes at the bass player, a tall thin boy with an unusually large Adam's apple. "Maybe I could date *him*— he's mysterious looking." She tried to clear her throat but broke into a hacking cough. "I think I'm getting sick. I must've caught something from Mike."

Andie rolled her eyes. Cindy had a boyfriend for a week when she was away this summer in Maine. He was the busboy at the Lobster Tale. "You only held hands," Andie whispered, poking Cindy playfully in the side.

Onstage, Kyle unplugged his guitar from the amp. As the band packed up their equipment, he strode over to their table, still smiling. "Hey." He sat down beside Andie. He was wearing a tattered blue CBGB shirt. "How'd you like the new songs?"

"They were great," she said, trying to steady her voice. "*You* were great." Andie kept staring at her hand, which was resting on the table only an inch away from his. She wanted him to grab it, to interlace his fingers in hers like they were a real couple.

She kept imagining herself standing in the crowd at one of Kyle's shows, the other groupies seething with jealousy as they realized he was staring at Andie, that every song was dedicated to her. She couldn't wait until Cate spotted them playing foosball in the den together and realized that Andie had something she didn't: a boyfriend. Under the table Kyle's knee knocked into the side of her leg and she flinched, suddenly nervous.

Kyle pulled his guitar into his lap. "It's awesome you came." He strummed slowly, covering the strings with one hand so it made a muted metallic sound. "What are you guys doing now? We're all going over to Mark's loft." Kyle nodded to the bassist, who had covered his shoulder-length blond hair with a backwards Mets cap. "You should come."

Andie looked at her watch, torn. It was already four, which meant in half an hour she had to be home and ready for her "date" with Clay Calhoun. If she was going to get back to the Upper East Side in time, she should've left five minutes ago. "We actually have to go. . . ." She sprang up from the table, pulling Cindy with her.

"Right." Kyle stared at his black and white–checked Vans, like she'd just told him she would rather spend the afternoon with the Haverford chess club. "Well, maybe I'll come over tomorrow? Lola mentioned you and your sisters were throwing a party?" He stopped strumming and looked up, waiting for Andie to fill in the sudden silence.

She tugged nervously on the highlight in her bangs. Kyle had already heard about the party. If she didn't invite him now, she could forget about him IMing her tonight, or tomorrow . . . or ever again. It didn't matter if she was supposed to be dating Clay, or if Lola had started straightening her hair just to impress Kyle. Kyle didn't know any of that. He would just think she hated him. "Yeah . . . you should come," she heard herself say.

Kyle pushed his sweaty bangs off his forehead and smiled. "Cool," he said. "See you then."

Andie swallowed hard, but her throat felt dry. She would hide out in her room if she had to, or fake a horrible stomach virus. She didn't *have* to go to the party. And now she *couldn't*—not with both Lola and Kyle there.

"You're completely insane," Cindy hissed, throwing her long jet-black hair over her shoulder. They turned down Madison Avenue, nearly knocking over a chubby-cheeked toddler who'd escaped from his mother. "When Lola sees you two together she's going to kill you."

It was a cool, breezy afternoon, but Andie's skin felt hot, like she'd gotten a second-degree sunburn. "What was I supposed to do? I couldn't not invite him."

Cindy shook her head. "You should have told him you weren't going to the party—anything. Now he's going to be there tomorrow, and so is Lola. She's going to figure out that you two have been talking. This is bad. Really, really bad." She let out a low cough. Cindy was great at making Andie feel like she was just as smart and talented as Cate, shooting mock fashion spreads on her Nikon Coolpix, or consoling her when the Ashton soccer team lost. But in crisis situations, she went into complete panic mode.

Cindy pulled off her fedora and smoothed down her hair. "You just have to tell Lola—she can't be mad at you. She's modeling for Gunther Gunta!"

"I tried," Andie mumbled. "There hasn't been a good time."

"Try again!" Cindy said, shaking her head. "She's going to know something is wrong when Kyle is wandering around the party looking for *you*." She blew Andie a kiss before taking off toward her apartment building, the Stagecoach, which had a blown-glass sculpture of a horse and buggy in the lobby.

Andie turned down Eighty-second Street. Cindy's words were still ringing in her ears when she spotted Clay in front of her town house. He was leaning against the wrought iron fence, kicking around a crumpled Coke can. "Sloane! Where you been?" he called.

Andie tried hard to smile, but couldn't. Right now Kyle was in a loft space in SoHo, probably talking about the Shins or playing Wii bowling with his bassist, Mark.

She pushed open the wrought iron gate. It felt like it weighed five hundred pounds. "Hey . . . sorry I'm late," she said, not feeling even the slightest bit sorry.

"No worries, yo. He pulled down his Yankees hat over his shaggy blond hair. "I told Brandon we were hanging out; he might come over later."

"Sure," Andie mumbled. "I love Brandon." The only thing worse than spending the afternoon with Clay was spending the afternoon with Clay *and* Brandon. They'd probably pants each other in the middle of the kitchen as Margot looked on in horror.

They walked into the foyer just as Lola was bounding down the stairs. She was wearing her red plaid Gap boxers and a Sherwood Academy sweatshirt. Her dirty blond hair looked just that—*dirty*. Instead of its usual dry, frizzy texture, it was greasy, like she'd washed it with vegetable oil. She looked from Clay to Andie, her green eyes bright. "Hello!" she said in her little British accent, a little too cheerfully.

Andie let out a deep breath, reminding herself that Lola was the reason Clay was over in the first place. As an aspiring model, Andie knew how to channel every emotion: happy, scared, mysterious, or bold. But today she'd be put to the ultimate test. Today she'd pretend she was in love . . . *with Clay Calhoun*. "Lola!" she said, winking behind Clay's back. "This is Clay." She singsonged the word *Clay*.

Lola smoothed down her red cloth headband. "Oh, hi! I've heard so much about you!" Clay's lips curled into a smile.

"Did you know Clay is one of the best players on the Haverford soccer team?" Andie asked. "You should tell Lola that story about you and Brandon at the Burger Joint." She punched Clay's arm playfully.

"Well," Clay started. "My friend and I had this contest to see who could eat the most burgers. Brandon upchucked on some tourist's shoes."

"Isn't he the funniest?" Andie cooed, staring into Clay's green eyes.

"Thanks, Sloane," he said, then he caught her hand and squeezed it tightly. She wanted to yank it away but he kept staring at her. Andie felt embarrassed for him, like she'd just caught him trimming his nose hair. It was easier to pretend she was his girlfriend when she thought of Clay as the boy who did bad Will Ferrell impressions and had every girl at Ashton checking his Facebook page five times a day. She didn't like being reminded that he *wasn't* pretending—that for him, this was *real*.

Lola smoothed down her headband, trying to imagine what it would be like to have someone look at her that way. Lately it felt like she only got noticed when she was doing something daft, like flashing her bum to an entire room of models. Even worse, when she'd invited Kyle to the party last night, he'd acted like she was a complete stranger. *Thanks 4 inviting me,* he'd written in the e-mail, *ur such a good friend.* She had wanted him to show up in one of his cute T-shirts and look at her the way Clay looked at Andie. Just for once, she wanted to know what it felt like to be seen.

"Are you coming to our party?" Lola asked, glancing from Andie to Clay.

"What party?" Clay turned to Andie. Her throat closed up. She couldn't breathe. She stepped back, behind Clay and shook her head, trying to get Lola's attention. But she just continued on.

"The party Saturday night. You have to come!" Lola clapped her hands together in front of her face. "We're going to have sweets and punch, and our sisters invited all these Haverford blokes."

"Sounds awesome," Clay said, looking from Lola to Andie. He furrowed his brows. "Why didn't you tell me about it, Sloane?"

Andie felt his eyes on her. "Lola . . . it's just . . ." she mumbled. "I kind of promised Cindy she could come."

"It doesn't matter," Lola cried. "Stella and Cate will never know if you invite one more guest."

"Right . . ." Andie muttered. She swallowed hard. Tomorrow night Clay, Kyle, and Lola would all be at the party, in her town house. Hiding from Kyle would've been hard, but hiding from Kyle, Lola, *and* Clay would be impossible.

TO: Lola Childs
FROM: Ayana Bennington
DATE: Friday, 5:02 p.m.
SUBJECT: Your contract with Gunther

Hi Lola,

I was delighted to hear your go-see went well. I had a feeling you'd be just the model Gunther was looking for. Which is why I'm writing . . .

I just spoke with Gunther regarding the contract. I understand his assistant gave you a copy for you and your guardian to sign. I wanted to stress, again, the fine print: You are not to bathe before the shoot. Apparently Gunther is very serious about this. He has a specific aesthetic he's going for with this campaign, so your cooperation is essential. Do call me Monday to let me know how everything went. Best of luck—I look forward to hearing from you.

All the best,
Ayana

DESPERATE TIMES CALL FOR SABOTAGING MEASURES

Cate looked out over the Great Lawn. It was covered with people, all reveling in one another's company. A group of boys tossed around a Frisbee while clusters of girls sat on blankets, picking Thai dumplings out of takeout containers. A man in baggy red sweatpants wheeled his hot dog cart past Cate, eyeing the stretch of empty bench beside her. "What are you looking at?" she snapped. The man sped up, glancing nervously over his shoulder at her.

She couldn't help it. She'd spent the entire afternoon without Stella—without anyone—and she'd never felt so self-conscious. Since fourth grade she'd never gone more than an hour or two without a friend beside her—especially not during the school year. She'd sit with the Chi Beta Phis at lunch, thankful she wasn't one of those people who ate solo, or she'd talk about how sad it was that Molly Lambert never had anyone to walk down the hall with. But today things had taken the kind of turn that made her believe in karma. Stella had taken Myra for her makeover, so

Cate had picked up gift bags for the party . . . alone. She'd called fifteen different caterers . . . alone. She'd even drafted the mass e-mail announcing Chi Sigma Mu's first official party by herself. Being friendless was awful. She felt like she'd left her house this morning and forgotten something essential—like her cell phone, her wallet, or her shirt.

She stared at her iPhone, willing it to ring. Stella was supposed to send picture messages of the makeover in progress: one as soon as they threaded off Mug's caterpillar 'stache, one after they cut her stringy blond hair, and a few of Mug trying on outfits for the party, so Cate could vote on which option she liked best. It was one thing to *talk* about making over Mug, but it was another thing to *do* it. Two hours had passed, and Cate still hadn't gotten confirmation that it was working.

Danny Plimpton bounded up the path. "Danny!" Cate cried, more grateful to see him than ever. With the exception of the woman at Papyrus, he was the only person she'd talked to all afternoon. "Sit! Please!" She patted the bench.

He raised one of his thick black eyebrows, as if he weren't certain he had the right Cate Sloane. Then he passed her a manila envelope. "It's all there, but I better run. The Eagle will be here any minute. I was right in front of him."

Cate dug into her black and white Balenciaga bag. "These are for you." She passed him a stack of things she'd found in Lola's desk. There was an English essay titled "My First Impressions of New York," a letter from a friend named Abby, and her Ashton Prep class schedule. While Lola was eating breakfast this morning Cate had snuck into her room and jotted down additional notes: *full name Lola Evelyn Childs, birthday July 31, plays the viola, has a stash of caramel candies in her nightstand, owns the complete works of Beethoven on CD.* "Lola will be at my party tomorrow, and you're officially invited. Just play it cool—don't talk to her too much or she'll know you like her."

"I won't." Danny ran his fingers over the papers as if they were made of gold. "Thanks, Cate." He took off, his black JanSport backpack swinging on one shoulder.

Cate peered into the folder, cringing at the first page. *I regret to inform you the date with Blythe Finley is confirmed. Tonight at 8. Jackson Hole.*

Ever since the basketball game, Cate couldn't think about Blythe without wanting to break something. Of course she'd gone after Eli—it was so typical of her. Last year, when Cate bought navy Tory Burch flats Blythe went out the next day and bought the same pair in black. When Cate decided to be a vegetarian for two weeks, Blythe started preaching about slaughterhouse conditions. So she had gotten a date with Eli first—that didn't mean it was going to be a *successful* date. At least not if Cate could help it.

She tucked the folder into her bag and pulled out *Catcher in the Rye*. She'd rolled the cover back and broken the spine so it looked like she'd read it five times.

"Hey, neighbor," a familiar voice called. Eli walked toward her, still in his blue Haverford warm-up pants.

Cate waved at him with the book. In the late-afternoon sun, Eli's flawless skin glistened with sweat. "Oh, you startled me. I was just reading."

Eli smiled at the cover. "That's my favorite book."

"Mine too." Cate leaned in close and raised an eyebrow. "So is that why you're in New York? You're a runaway from some boarding school?"

"I wish my life were that exciting." Eli laughed. "I can't even find my way out of Central Park, let alone to some cheap hotel. Mind if I follow you home?"

You can follow me anywhere, Cate thought, as she let her shoulder graze his. They started down the path toward the Met, the trees forming a canopy of leaves above their heads. Everywhere Cate looked people were paired off. On the path in front of them, an elderly couple held hands, their backs hunched with age. A little girl with pigtails shared her lollipop with a buck-toothed boy. Even the dogs were in heat. On the grass outside the Temple of Dendur, a golden retriever licked frantically at a poodle's butt.

For the first time all afternoon, Cate felt at ease. She wasn't walking around alone, pretending she was having a super-important conversation on her iPhone. She was walking with *Eli Punch*, his hand swinging inches from hers. They were together, and she was *someone* again. "Good game yesterday," she said finally.

"I looked for you afterward, but it was so packed I couldn't find you." Eli pushed his thick black hair off his forehead.

"I saw Blythe Finley there." Cate paused when she said Blythe's name, waiting for a smirk or a scrunch of the nose—anything that would reveal how Eli felt. But there was nothing. "She told me you guys are going out tonight?"

"Yeah." Eli just shrugged. "I met her and her friends in Sheep Meadow the other day." Cate cringed at those words: *her and her friends*. Priya and Sophie weren't Blythe's friends—they were prisoners of war. "I guess she knows some of the guys on the basketball team. She seems cool."

Cate punted a rock with her Sigerson Morrison flat, sending it skittering down the path. When she and Stella had been fighting over who would be Chi Beta Phi's president, Stella had impressed her friends by introducing them to the entire Haverford varsity basketball team. Cate knew that was going to come back to haunt her, like the fourth-grade yearbook picture where she'd sneezed.

They turned up Fifth Avenue past the Met, where a man stood selling roses for a dollar. Cate glanced at Eli, hoping he'd pluck one from the bunch and hand it to her, but they just kept walking.

Cate clenched her fists as she imagined Blythe and Eli snuggled in a corner of Jackson Hole, feeding each other spoonfuls of strawberry ice cream. Eli had to know that there wasn't anything "cool" about Blythe. She would use him just like she used Cate—to get to the top. "You know . . . I was good friends with Blythe. But then I realized a few things about her."

Eli furrowed his dark brows. "What kinds of *things*?"

"Well," Cate searched her memory. She had nearly ten years of history with Blythe. There were more than enough "things" to bring up. "Once she stole a Ralph Lauren bracelet from Bloomingdale's. It was really sketchy." So that wasn't exactly the truth. Blythe had tried on the bracelet and forgotten about it, walking home with it on her wrist. Then she was too embarrassed to take it back. It was an accident—but it was still, technically, stealing.

"That's really weird. . . ." Eli tucked his thumbs under his backpack straps.

Cate was going for disturbing, unforgivable, or messed up—not *weird*. Weird wasn't enough to stop Eli from liking Blythe. "And that's not all," Cate could feel the words spilling one by one from her mouth. "Once she kicked a golden Lab puppy. We were walking down Madison and—boom!" Cate mimed punting a football. Eli flinched. "Right. In. The. Head."

Eli raised his eyebrows in shock. "I know . . ." Cate continued. "That poor . . . creature." Cate nodded solemnly. If she wanted to get into specifics, Blythe really *tripped* over the puppy, which was running around the sidewalk in circles, chasing its tail. But Cate could've sworn she saw her Juicy wedge knock it in the head.

Cate turned down Eighty-second Street, a bounce in her step. She'd spent half her summer lying on her roof deck with Blythe, planning ninth grade. They were supposed to take a train trip to visit Priya's sister Veena at Yale. They were supposed to spend Saturday nights in Sophie's hot tub, and Sunday mornings choreographing their dance for the Ashton talent show. Cate was supposed to be with the Chi Beta Phis, but Blythe betrayed her. Every moment they'd talked, every hug, every laugh—it was all a lie. From now on, all bets were off. "And this is just gross, but once she went a whole week without brushing her teeth."

Cate paused in front of her town house watching as Eli shook his head in disgust. Maybe Sophie had dared Blythe not to brush her teeth, but that was just a *minor* detail. "By the way," Cate added, staring into Eli's dark eyes. "My sisters and I are having a party tomorrow night. You should come."

His lips curled into a smile. "I'll be there." Then he bounded up his stoop, his keys jingling in his hand. He paused for a moment before heading inside. "And thanks for warning me about Blythe."

"No problem." Cate squeezed her hands together as he disappeared inside. Tomorrow Eli would be in *her* house, at *her* party, as *her* date. They'd sit alone in the candlelit garden and Cate would casually mention how she'd played the lead in *Annie* and *South Pacific,* and how she'd been class president three years in a row. She'd make a joke about the Haverford basketball team, mentioning how they were all, literally, players. *I'm not like that,* Eli would say, his perfect pink lips moving closer and closer to hers. They'd finally kiss, not bothering to stop until the party was over, until one by one the guests filed out and everyone—including Blythe—was gone.

FRIENDS DON'T LET FRIENDS BE CALLED "SLUG"

"I've never been in here before," Myra said, glancing around the fifth floor of Saks Fifth Avenue. A crystal chandelier hung over the Elie Tahari section, illuminating three mannequins in evening gowns. "It's so . . . *glamorous*."

Stella and Myra's arms were piled high with Theory sweaters, Nanette Lepore dresses, and Marc by Marc Jacobs skirts, as though they were having a contest to see who could carry the most designer apparel. "I haven't been here either," Stella said. "It reminds me a little of Harrods." Stella squeezed the clothes to her chest, thinking of the sweets counter in the massive London department store. It was packed with dark chocolate hearts, caramels, and yogurt-covered pretzels. She sometimes spent a half hour there, just trying to pick out truffles.

They approached the racks of Diane von Furstenberg dresses, and Stella rested her heap of clothing on the register. Behind it, a woman with over-lined lips was turned around, trying to inconspicuously pick a piece of pesto from her teeth. "Why, hello!" she cried a little too loudly, suddenly realizing Myra and Stella were there. She rang up the items one by one.

Just then, Stella's mobile buzzed. "Who is it?" Myra asked. She tried to peek at the screen, but Stella pulled it closer to her chest as she read the message.

CATE: SO?!?!? HOW'S THE MAKEOVER GOING??!?! WHERE R THE PICS?!?!?

"It's Cate—she's excited you're our Mu," Stella lied. She'd secretly taken a photo of Myra after her haircut and one when she came out of the dressing room in her navy blue Marc Jacobs shirtdress, but she couldn't bring herself to actually send them to Cate. She didn't want her making any judgments based on some grainy mobile pictures—too much was at stake. Myra knew they had to get ready for tomorrow's party, but she didn't know that if she wasn't ready . . . she was out. And Stella would hear, for the next ten years of her life, how she'd ruined Chi Sigma.

Myra laughed. "I never would've thought I'd be friends with Cate Sloane. Ever." Whenever she smiled her brown eyes folded up in the corners, giving her momentary crow's feet.

Stella tried hard to smile. Technically, they weren't friends . . . *yet*. She imagined Cate circling Myra, appraising her like a Sotheby's antique. She'd inspect her cuticles and check for split ends, trying to decide if Stella had done a thorough enough makeover.

As the sales clerk rang up the last Diane von Furstenberg dress, Stella slid her AmEx gold card across the counter. "The total is—"

"Wait," a voice interrupted. Stella turned to see Blythe, with Sophie and Priya standing close behind her, all still in their gray uniform skirts. Blythe leveled her gray eyes at Stella as she threw a handful of plastic packages onto the counter. "You forgot *these*."

Each one of the colorful sleeves displayed a glittery mesh thong. Stella froze, feeling like she'd swallowed a bowling ball. She hadn't seen Cloud McClean's face since last year, when Lola accidentally stumbled on her video "Love Cancer" on MTV. But there she was, winking at Stella from the front of each package, her white-blond hair styled in a sultry up-do.

"Did you want these?" the sales clerk asked, holding a fuchsia one up.

Stella stared at the package. Cloud McClean—unitard-wearing, glitter thong–endorsing, father-stealing Cloud McClean—had showed up in her life last year like a grenade, blowing her family apart. Every time Stella felt free, forgetful, Cloud appeared. There was no escaping her, even in New York, in a department store thousands of miles away from London.

Myra plucked the thong out of the woman's hand and scooped the rest into her arms. Her face was contorted in anger, like someone had just stomped on Pythagoras' tail for fun. "Absolutely not," she snapped. "These are made by trash, for trash. The only person buying them is *you*." She shoved them back into Blythe's arms.

Blythe's face turned a deep pink. "Whatever . . . Mug," she muttered, obviously flustered. Blythe turned on her Tory Burch heel. She threw the glitter thongs onto a Theory table, toppling a tower of baby blue sweaters.

Stella grabbed Myra's arm. She'd never seen Blythe speechless before. "Thanks," she mumbled as the sales clerk swiped her card.

They both watched as Blythe and the Beta Sigma Phis disappeared down the escalator. "No problem," Myra said. "I know how it feels to be teased."

Stella suddenly felt the urge to apologize—for everything. Maybe she'd never called Myra "Mug the Slug" to her face, but she'd definitely laughed when other people did. She'd spent so much time staring at Myra's bleached mustache, or rolling her eyes at her Don't Drink and Derive key chain, she never noticed that Myra was funny . . . and genuinely nice. When every other Ashton girl was treating Stella like toxic waste, Myra sat next to her at lunch and was thrilled to be her lab partner.

Myra looped her arm through Stella's. "Let's go." They took off toward the escalator, the shopping bags swinging on their arms. "I have my first fashion show to put on."

"Voilà!" Myra said, throwing Stella's closet door open in a dramatic reveal. Her blond hair was tucked neatly behind her ears, showing off two hammered gold hoops. The blue Diane von Furstenberg wrap dress looked like it had been custom tailored to her petite frame. As she spun around she looked prettier than Blythe, prettier than any of the girls at Ashton Prep who had laughed at her.

"You're brilliant!" Stella cried. Myra spun around and her skirt flared out, exposing her rainbow knee-highs. Stella's eyes settled on Myra's toes, each one snuggled into its own colored pouch.

"Oh," Myra followed Stella's gaze. "I guess I should throw these away . . ."

"No," Stella shook her head, smiling. She couldn't tell Myra to get rid of them. It would be like telling Cindy Crawford to get rid of her mole. "Definitely not. They're so . . . *you*."

"Well, maybe I'll wear them under my new jeans from now on." Myra smiled at her reflection in the full-length mirror on Stella's door. "Oh my gosh. The Mathletes are going to die when they see me."

Stella laughed, imagining Myra swarmed by guys clutching protractors and pads of graph paper. Just then, there was a knock on the door. Stella opened it a crack.

Cate was standing in the hall, looking like she was about to break down the door. "Um . . . remember me?" she hissed. "What happened? Where is she?"

Stella glanced back at Myra. She was standing in the center of the room, smoothing down her blond bob. She was as ready as she'd ever be. "I give you . . . Myra Granberry: our Mu." She flung the door open.

"Hi," Myra said shyly.

Cate took in a deep breath, feeling like she'd been trapped underwater and only now come up for air. Stella had been right. Myra *was* Chi Sigma material; she'd just needed a little help. Her pale skin was flawless, and her cheekbones were dusted with a pale pink blush. Now that they'd transformed her into a Chloë Sevigny look-alike, there was nothing Chi Sigma couldn't do. "You look amazing!" Cate cried. Myra's face broke into a smile. Cate rested her hands on her hips and surveyed her one last time. "Welcome to Chi Sigma, Slug!"

Stella watched Myra's face fall, her brown eyes suddenly dull. It was the same face Stella had seen that day in the drawing room, when Cate made fun of her facial hair. "Cate," she said through clenched teeth. "Can I talk to you outside for a minute?"

"What?" Cate shrugged, her dark brown hair falling in her face.

Stella pulled Cate into the hallway, shutting the door behind them. "If Myra is going to be in Chi Sigma, you can't keep on like that."

"Like what?" Cate stared at the ceiling, like she was searching for the answer somewhere beyond the crown molding.

"No more Mug the Slug talk—no more calling her fugly mugly. She's one of us now." Stella rested her hands on her hips. Even if she and Cate were the original members of the sorority, there needed to be some ground rules. She didn't make over Myra so Cate could torture her for the rest of the year.

Cate picked at her red nail polish. "Fine. But just do me a favor. Make sure she doesn't ramble on about coordinate planes at the party tomorrow. I don't want her embarrassing me in front of Eli." Then she took off down the narrow staircase.

"She won't!" Stella called. "You're going to thank me!" She crept back into the room. Myra was sitting on the edge of Stella's queen bed, knocking her heels against the black footboard. "Myra, I'm sorry. She didn't mean that."

"It's fine," Myra mumbled. But Stella could tell it wasn't fine. Myra's forehead was scrunched in concentration, like she was trying hard not to cry.

Don't, Stella thought. *Do not cry.* She wanted to tell Myra that

Cate was hard on everyone. She'd said Lola needed to gain two stone, she'd said Andie needed growth hormones, and every time she looked at Heath Bar she turned away in disgust, calling him "that morbidly obese thing." She wanted to tell Myra that just last week *she* was taking insults from Cate Sloane, who'd all but ordered her to go back to London. If you were going to survive her friendship there was one rule to follow: Take nothing personally.

"Please don't worry about Cate. She's just a little . . . temperamental," Stella finally offered. Maybe *temperamental* wasn't quite the right word, but Stella didn't want Myra thinking Cate was an awful person. They still had to be friends. "Now I have one more surprise for you. I was saving it for the party but . . ." She went into her walk-in closet, gesturing for Myra to follow her. She pulled a Saks box off the top shelf. "This is for you."

Myra tucked her hair behind her ears, staring at the black and white box, tied with a red silk bow. "This is for me?" she asked, her brown eyes wide.

"I thought you might like it." Stella grinned, squeezing Myra's shoulder.

Myra opened the box and held the Marc Jacobs bag in the air like it was a trophy. "It has my initials on it!" She cried, running her fingers over the letters *M.G.* While Myra was getting fitted for new bras, Stella had picked out the hobo bag and gotten it embossed—without the *U*, to free her of her nickname. It was the perfect new alternative to her L.L. Bean knapsack. "Oh my gosh!" She threw her arms around Stella, pulling her into hug. "This is the nicest thing anyone has ever done for me."

Stella hoped she was exaggerating, but as Myra squeezed her tight she had the sinking feeling she wasn't. In the last three hours Myra's mobile hadn't rung once. No one had texted to see where she was, or what her plans were for Friday night. Every lunch period Stella watched her from across the cafeteria as Myra sat alone, reading a beaten-up copy of Plato's *Republic*. It was as if Myra had spent years at Ashton Prep as a ghost, roaming the halls friendless, visible only to teachers, Mathletes, and anyone looking for someone to torment.

"You deserve it," Stella said, smiling. "You're a good friend." She thought about Blythe's smug face, and the glitter thongs, and how Myra had jumped to defend her, more loyal than a guard dog. Out of all the things she'd told Myra that afternoon—*you look great in red, green shadow complements your eyes, you should always wear earrings*—that statement was the most true.

TO: CSMGuestList@gmail.com
FROM: Cate Sloane
CC: Stella Childs
DATE: Friday, 5:33 p.m.
SUBJECT: Chi Sigma Mu Mixer

You've watched. You've waited.
You've wondered.
And now . . . you won't believe your eyes.

Join Ashton Prep's hottest new sorority as we
induct our third member:

Myra Granberry

Chi Sigma Mu Mixer
This Saturday, 8 p.m.
The Sloane town house
50 East 82nd Street
Refreshments will be served.
Parents will be gone.
Be there or be jealous.

THE SMELL OF SUCCESS

Friday night, the waiter at Tao set a bowl of velvet-corn-and-crab soup in front of Lola, trying with the other hand to inconspicuously cover his nose. Lola sank lower in her chair, glancing around the table at her sisters and her grandmum to see if anyone had noticed. The last thing she wanted to do was go anywhere in public, but her grandmum had insisted on taking them out for dinner. That afternoon a cab had splashed electric green gutter water all over her. At first she was convinced it would make her "guttaaa" shoot more authentic, but four hours later she smelled like a foul mixture of turpentine and old bologna.

Lola pulled her sweatshirt close to her neck. She'd tried to cover up the stench by wearing a freshly washed Gap hoodie, but it seemed like anyone who came within a one-foot radius of her needed a gas mask.

At the other end of the table, Margot adjusted her pea-size hearing aid and winked at Lola. She'd signed the release form for the Gunther Gunta shoot, insisting Emma would be thrilled that

Lola was modeling. But when her mum rang yesterday from Tahiti and Lola tried to tell her about it, the connection kept breaking up. Lola imagined her on a beach somewhere with Winston, sipping drinks with those silly umbrellas in them. She wanted her mum to be happy, she did, but she wanted her to be happy in New York. She needed her *here,* to tell her about the time she modeled in the Atlantic Ocean in January, or had to walk down the runway dressed in an alligator-skin evening gown, her face painted neon green. She was the only person who could understand.

"Cheers!" Margot hooted to the girls, holding up her dirty martini. "Here's to my date with Walter Hodgeworth." She took a swig of the murky liquid.

Stella let out a deep breath, not bothering to lift her Diet Coke. It was bad enough that her grandmum wore leather pants to dinner, even though she had a serious case of pancake bum. But now she'd spent half an hour keeping on about Walter's "young physique." Stella glanced around the crowded restaurant, taking in a sixteen-foot Buddha towering over a reflecting pool with live carp. Two tables over, a group of *Sex and the City* wannabes discussed their dating escapades a little too loudly.

Just then three waiters circled the table, dropping plates of Dragon Tail spareribs and Thai crab cakes. "I already got thirty-one responses to the invite," Cate whispered to Stella as she plunged her knife into her soy ginger–glazed salmon. "Betsy Carmichael wants to cover Myra's makeover for Ashton News." Cate put emphasis on the word *Myra,* as if to say, *See? I'm trying.* "She even wants to do an exclusive interview on my split from Chi Beta Phi."

Stella stuck a lobster dumpling in her mouth and practically swallowed it whole. She was starting to feel like she was going through her own split. Pippa and Bridget had finally e-mailed, but only to announce that Bridget had highlighted her red hair and Pippa was now dating Robin Lawrence, who—just last spring—was someone *Stella* fancied. They'd signed the e-mail "Miss you!" even though they hadn't asked about her new school, or Winston, or anything really. Their lives in London were barreling on, without Stella, and it felt like they didn't even care. "We saw Blythe in Saks today," Stella mentioned.

But Cate didn't respond. She was eyeing her plate suspiciously, her nose scrunched up like she'd just gotten a whiff of cheap perfume. "I think my salmon is bad." Cate raised her dainty hand in the air, signaling for the waiter.

Lola felt like she was sitting on a heating vent. From across the table Andie stared at her, her brown eyes wide. Stella and Cate didn't know about Gunther—and it was better that way. The last thing she wanted was Cate listing all the reasons why she wasn't qualified to be a model, or Stella blabbing it to their mum the next time she called from Tahiti. Lola wanted to be the one to tell her.

"I'm sure it's brilliant," Lola insisted a little too loudly. But the waiter was already there.

"The salmon doesn't smell right," Cate said, pushing the fish with her fork. She offered the plate to the waiter, but he didn't take it.

Instead, he narrowed his beady eyes at Lola. "I'm sorry," he said, shaking his head. "But it's not the salmon."

Lola pulled her hoodie tighter around her, trying to conceal the stench. But Cate was already leaning in, sniffing her like she was a container of yogurt that was past its expiration date. "Lola, is that *you*?"

At the other end of the table, Margot tried to change the subject. "Did I mention Walter ran a marathon last year? He's *very* active." She patted down her stiff blond hair.

"Lola," Stella hissed, grabbing her sister's arm and lifting it up. "You smell like a rubbish bin!"

"All right, luvs, let's not make a scene." Margot let out an uncomfortable laugh. At the table next to them a couple in their forties watched in horror as Stella stuck her nose in Lola's armpit.

"You're dirtier than Margot's martini," Cate said. Stella laughed loudly and a few other tables turned to look. "You better take a shower before tomorrow. I don't want you stinking up my"—she glanced quickly at Margot—"*town house.*"

Lola's nose twitched as she pushed farther away from the table. She knew Cate was talking about the bloody party, but she didn't care about it anymore. Kyle was online earlier, but when she'd asked him if he was actually coming tomorrow night he'd signed off. She pictured him cuddled up on a love seat, watching *Harry Potter and the Goblet of Fire* with Imaginary Girl, holding her tight during the scariest part, when Harry is in the graveyard with Voldemort. *I love the way you smell,* he'd whisper, breathing in her Clinique Happy perfume.

Andie watched as Lola's eyes brimmed with tears. She'd noticed the stench too, but knew better than to say anything.

Last night, Lola confessed that part of the Gunther Gunta shoot involved not showering. While Andie washed her face Lola stood three feet away from the sink, as though she were the Wicked Witch of the West and would melt if she got a drop of water on her. "She can't take a shower," she finally said, unable to stand it any longer. Maybe Lola hadn't wanted to tell them, but the only way to shut Cate up was to impress her. "Because *Gunther Gunta* told her not to—heard of him? Lola is modeling for him tomorrow." She glanced at Lola and smiled.

Cate pointed a finger in Lola's face. "*You're* modeling for *Gunther Gunta?*"

"Yes," Andie said proudly, answering the question for her.

Lola sat up a little straighter. Even if she smelled like a kitty litter box, there was something satisfying about Cate's reaction. Mainly that she was having one. She only talked to Lola to complain about Heath Bar puking chunks of Fancy Feast in her new Botkier bag. When they were in the kitchen together, or the den—or anywhere—Cate barely said a word, moving around her like she wasn't even there.

"Wow, Lola," Stella said quietly. "Why didn't you tell me?"

"Please don't say anything to Mum," Lola whispered to Stella. "I want it to be a surprise." Last week, Emma had spent so much time planning the wedding Lola had barely seen her. Growing up, her mum was always busy with work, but now it was even worse. She had a new contract with Ralph Lauren, she had a new husband, and she had two new daughters. Lola couldn't wait for her to come home from the honeymoon so they could be alone. She would show her the photos from the shoot and they'd talk about Gunther and his silly accent. Maybe they'd even be on Ralph Lauren billboards together—as mother-and-daughter models.

Stella pinched her nose as she popped a lobster dumpling in her mouth. "Oh she'll be surprised." Her voice sounded like she had a cold. "But you have to take a shower. Otherwise we're going to quarantine you."

"Let's just eat, okay?" Andie said, taking a bite of her spare ribs. Cate rolled her eyes in protest, but eventually everyone returned to their dinners.

Lola let out a deep breath, relieved. She didn't care if Cate called her Dumpster Diva or Stella forced her to wear a plastic hazmat suit around the town house. It didn't matter. Only one person's opinion counted: Gunther Gunta's. And tomorrow, with his help, she'd be a supermodel.

Late that night, Lola was twisted up in her blankets, unable to sleep. When she'd walked into her room after dinner, Heath Bar had hissed and darted under the bed, like she was a burglar with bad hygiene. The stench had now taken on a slight seafood odor, probably a side effect of her corn-and-crab soup. It was so awful she'd tried to stuff her nose with earplugs, but they kept falling out.

She rolled around, finally pulling her shower cap off. She'd hoped it would keep her pillowcases clean, but now her roots were slicked with sweat. Her leg was itching badly like it did when she'd gotten stung by a jellyfish in Mykonos.

Nooo baaathing. Gunther's voice echoed in her head. *One*

with the guttaaaa. She dug her nails into her calf and scratched the spot, but it felt even worse. She flipped on her bedside lamp and went into the loo, staring at the white claw-foot tub. She could just wash her leg and go back to bed. Just her leg. Gunther wouldn't be able to tell that her calf was any less "feelthy" than the rest of her.

She ran the bath and stepped in, hiking her pajama pants up to her knee. The warm water ran over her shin. She lathered up her hands, smelling the sweet scent of the Bath & Body Works Cucumber Melon body wash. *No baaathing!* The voice said again. She imagined Gunther Gunta with his arms crossed over his chubby belly, staring disapprovingly at her through the thick lenses of his glasses. *One with the guttaaaa!!*

She knew she shouldn't—she couldn't. But the body wash smelled so inviting, and the warm water felt so nice on her skin. She peeled off her pajamas and tossed them on the floor. With one quick turn of the tap the shower started, rinsing away the nasty green gutter water, the crab soup, and the horrible stench that had been following her around all day. *I zed no baaaathing!* the voice hissed. But Lola ignored it as she inhaled the fresh scent of Andie's rosemary mint Aveda shampoo. Showering felt *too* good. Tomorrow, before the shoot, she'd just have to find another way to be *one with tha guttaaa.*

TO: Cindy Ng
FROM: Andie Sloane
DATE: Saturday, 9:46 a.m.
SUBJECT: Party tonight . . .

Umm . . . new development on the Lola front. I was going to tell her about Kyle, I was, but then she told Clay to come tonight . . . as my date. So I can't back out of the party now.

Can you please (seriously I'm begging you, please) distract Lola when Kyle gets here? Clay has to leave to go to the Ludacris concert with Brandon. You'd only have to keep her in her room for an hour or so while I hang out with Kyle.

Andie

TO: Andie Sloane
FROM: Cindy Ng
DATE: Saturday, 11:08 p.m.
SUBJECT: Re: Party tonight . . .

Ugh. I just woke up and I feel like I've been run over by a bus. My nose is stuffed up, I still have that awful cough, and I get dizzy whenever I stand up too fast. If you need me to come, I'll come, but you may have to push me around in a wheelchair.

xoxox
Cindy

PS: I still think you're being insane. Just tell her the truth!

PARTING IS SUCH SWEET SORROW

Stella bounded down the stairs, skipping every other step. She was supposed to meet Myra at Bliss for manicures and pedicures, and she was running late. Last night after dinner, she'd spent an hour in Barneys, picking out a pair of kitten heels to go with Myra's new dress. As she circled the shoe section for the fourth time, trying to decide if Myra would think feathered Manolo Blahniks were tacky, she suddenly realized: Myra hadn't even *worn* heels before. She was the complete opposite of any girl Stella had ever been friends with, and lately that felt like a very good thing.

After the e-mail from Bridget and Pippa, Stella couldn't stop thinking about their "friendship." When the rag mags posted a picture of Stella's mum crying after the divorce Stella had spent a whole weekend in Bridget's room. She'd been furious, only to discover the same magazine under Bridget's bed. When she broke her arm at the Kew Gardens ice rink, Lola was the one who ran for help. Pippa and Bridget just stood there giggling, convinced she was putting them on. Now Stella kept picturing that moment in Saks—with Blythe—and imagining what Pippa and Bridget would've said if *they'd* been there. The only answer she could come up with was . . . nothing.

Stella turned down the hall and raced toward the wide mahogany staircase. "Perfect timing!" Cate's voice called as she emerged from the den. "Can you be ready in ten?" She glanced at the notebook in her hand. "We need to go to Dylan's Candy Bar to get the M&M's, and I want to make a banner that says 'Chi Sigma Mu.' Then, I was thinking of getting a few Polaroid cameras, that way everyone can take pictures. Which reminds me—we'll need somewhere for people to post them . . ." She trailed off, scribbling something in the book. "Maybe a corkboard or something? Is that too lame?" She chewed on the end of her pencil and stared at Stella.

"That sounds . . . brilliant," Stella finally said. She glanced down at the shoe box in her hands. "But I made plans today with Myra. I should've met her five minutes ago." She thought she and Cate had an unspoken agreement—Stella would prepare Myra for the party, and Cate would do everything else. Divide and conquer.

"Myra?" Cate snapped. "I told you. She looks amazing. Job well done. Now we have more important things to do." She dug her thumbnail into the pencil, feeling the wood give. The whole point of Chi Sigma Mu was so she had a new group of friends— two people who could calm her down before musical auditions or tell her when she was being too mean to Andie. People who would stand beside her when Blythe, Sophie, and Priya passed in the hall, staring her down like she was some sort of juvenile delinquent, out on parole. She didn't found the sorority so she could plan parties alone. "Just cancel." Stella winced, as though that weren't an option. "Or invite her to come with us. Whatever. I *need* you."

Stella imagined Myra waiting in the lobby of Bliss, nervously checking her mobile. They'd been so busy with the makeover, Stella had decided that today they would just relax. Myra would get her first pedicure, and they'd go to brunch at Sarabeth's—the cozy restaurant Stella kept passing on Madison Avenue that always smelled of pancakes. Stella planned on talking to her about Bridget and Pippa, and maybe even debrief her about Cate, who was bound to call Myra "Mug" again, or obsessively watch her upper lip like a Chia Pet, waiting for signs of growth. You could take the girl out of Chi Beta Phi, but you couldn't take the Chi Beta Phi out of the girl. "I promised her I'd be there," Stella said slowly.

Cate stood frozen. "You're serious?" she asked.

"I'll help you this afternoon. Promise." Stella offered a weak smile. If she had any chance of making her pedicure appointment she had to leave now. She headed down the stairs, glancing over her shoulder at Cate. "I'll be back so soon. It's not a big deal." But as she darted through the foyer and out the door, she couldn't shake the feeling that to Cate, it was.

Just being in Dylan's Candy Bar gave Cate a stomachache. There were giant plastic lollipops stacked to the ceiling, bar stools designed to look like peppermint candies, and every wall was a rainbow of jelly beans, gummi bears, and M&M's. Cate *hated* sweets. She hated chocolate cake, oatmeal raisin cookies, lemon drops, and anything else with sugar in it. And right now she hated Stella for making her come to this Willy Wonka crack den alone.

After Stella left for Bliss, Cate had sat in the den, feeling more rejected than a tone-deaf cross-dresser on *American Idol*. She'd reviewed her to-do list and tried to estimate how long, exactly, it would take Stella to get there, have a manicure and pedicure, and get back. But after two hours and not one single text, she'd finally given up and left. The M&M's weren't going to customize themselves.

Cate stood at the end of a long line of tourists, their arms piled with candy bars, Disney Pez dispensers, and tins of malt balls. A little girl with a sparkly DIVA shirt sucked on a rainbow-swirl lollipop the size of her head. Cate turned away, disgusted by her sticky blue mouth. That's when she spotted them. In the back corner, eating ice cream sundaes at a table by the window, were Blythe, Priya, and Sophie. They were laughing.

Sophie pulled her plastic spoon back and aimed, as though she were about to launch some chocolate ice cream right in Blythe's face. "Don't you dare, Sophie!" Blythe hooted, so loudly the people at the next table turned to watch. Cate tried to hide behind a spinning rack of candy bars. It was bad enough she had walked down all of Third Avenue alone—the last thing she needed was Beta Sigma Phis knowing.

"Do it!" Priya yelled, egging Sophie on.

Blythe was smiling as she pushed her chair farther and

farther from the table. "I swear, Sophie. You better not." Cate gazed longingly at the empty seat beside them. Just a few weeks ago Sophie was chasing *her* around with a glass of Crystal Light, threatening to pour it over her head. Once she'd waited under Cate's bed for a whole hour, only to scare her half to death by grabbing her ankles. Sophie's immaturity always seemed like this annoying thing Cate had to put up with, but now she missed it most. It made everything—sleepovers, brunch, or just gym class—more fun.

Sophie finally turned the spoon on herself, launching the ice cream into her mouth. As she wiped her lips with a napkin she noticed Cate peering out from behind the candy bar rack. Priya and Blythe both followed her gaze.

Cate picked up some peanut brittle and read the nutrition label, feeling like she'd just gotten caught spying on them through Priya's bedroom window. It didn't matter if she was alone—they had already seen her. And if she didn't want to look like some sort of creepy Peeping Tom, she needed to save face immediately.

She took a deep breath and strolled over to the table. "I thought that was you guys," she called, trying to sound breezy. She rested her hand on the back of the empty chair. Even if she'd wandered around alone all morning, she'd spent the last three years in the Ashton drama club. Acting was something she knew how to do. "I was just shopping for some candy for tonight. Everyone's calling it the biggest party of the year. I can't believe all the e-mails I've gotten." Cate shrugged, trying to seem breezy.

"Why are *you* shopping for candy?" Blythe narrowed her

gray eyes at Cate. "You hate candy. Where's Mug and Stella?" She glanced around the store. Two little boys were doped up on sugar and chasing each other through the chocolate section.

Cate swallowed hard. When Cate was friends with the Chi Beta Phis, they knew each other's whereabouts at all times. Priya sent a mass text when she broke her foot at gymnastic practice and had to go to the St. Vincent's emergency room. Sophie had written regular e-mail updates from the Hamptons last summer, complaining of her grandmother's bridge and pinochle parties. And Blythe and Cate kept in the best touch. When they weren't physically together, they called each other three times a day to consult on Barneys purchases, or gossip about Eleanor Donner's germaphobia, or talk about how Cate's dad was acting like a seventh-grader with a bad crush. But it was different with Stella. She and Mug (correction—*Myra*) could have been on a British Airways flight back to London at that very moment. Cate had no idea. Sometimes it felt like Stella didn't even need her. "There's so much to do for tonight, we had to split up. Myra and Stella really didn't want to, but I insisted."

"Well, let's hope Myra's up to par for the party." Priya dug her spoon into her banana split. "Our sneak preview yesterday still left much to be desired."

"She will be," Cate said. "Don't worry." She stood there a moment longer, trying to remind herself that Blythe had gone out on a date with Eli last night. *Her* Eli. She told herself, again, that Priya and Sophie were like sheep, following anyone who would lead. The three of them were *not* her friends anymore— they were dead weight.

"Is that all?" Blythe asked. She glanced at Cate's hands, which were still holding on to the back of the empty chair.

"No," Cate snapped, letting go. She straightened up, searching for the right words. She wasn't going to let Blythe Finley, spray-tan addict, decide when the conversation was over. "I wanted to offer my condolences in advance. Tonight is Beta Sigma Phi's funeral." She watched Blythe's face harden. Priya threw her spoon into her sundae as Sophie squeezed a fistful of her flattened brown hair. With that, Cate stalked off toward the register. There was something satisfying about threatening Blythe. She just wished she was completely convinced of it herself.

Saturday afternoon, Stella rapped her knuckles on Cate's door for the third time and still, no one answered. She finally pushed it open. Three Cynthia Rowley dresses were strewn over her bed, along with a Jenga-like tower of shoe boxes. But Cate wasn't there.

She whipped out her mobile. As she texted away, she remembered Cate's face before she left for Bliss, feeling the slightest pang of guilt. Her blue eyes had been wide, like those of a puppy who was being abandoned at the pound.

STELLA: JUST GOT BACK! WHERE R U? READY TO GO GET CANDY?

She felt like a member of the CIA, sending encoded messages. The translation being: READY TO FORGIVE ME? She hoped the answer was yes.

Stella was as excited as Cate was, she just wasn't worried about silly details like customized M&M's and Polaroid cameras. She and Cate already had the two ingredients every good party needed: a parentless town house and fabulous hosts. And because of Stella's good work, there were now *three* of them.

Her iPhone buzzed.

CATE: LIVING ROOM

Stella bounded down the stairs. As she strolled into the living room, she could hear the squeaky sound of markers on poster board. Behind the couch, Cate was finishing a Chi Sigma Mu banner, complete with the Greek letters. Tiny pink bags were piled up around her, CHI SIGMA MU printed on their fronts. She looked up at Stella, her pale face tense with worry. "Well look who decided to help out. Did you shut the door? We can't let Margot see this."

Stella swallowed hard, eyeing the gift bags. Cate had obviously started the party planning without her. "I'm ready to go to Dylan's Candy Bar . . ." she said in a small voice.

"Don't worry about it," Cate muttered. "I already went. *And* I picked up the cupcakes from Magnolia Bakery *and* the Polaroid cameras *and* I'm making the banner. Everything is done." Cate pressed down hard on the magenta marker, coloring in the last of the *U*. She couldn't stop thinking about what had happened at Dylan's Candy Bar, how Blythe, Priya, and Sophie had all looked so happy without her. Even if Blythe had staged a coup last week, she never would've chosen some hairy Mathlete over Cate. She'd been there for every moment in Cate's life—since forever. When Cate cried on her first day of kindergarten, Blythe gave her her Polly Pocket to play with. Blythe was Cate's campaign manager during the eighth-grade election, and when Cate met Emma for the first time Blythe was standing right next to her, squeezing Cate's hand twice to secretly tell her she approved. Maybe Blythe had competed with her for the Chi Beta Phi presidency and for Eli too—but when they'd been friends, they'd actually been friends.

"Cate," Stella continued. "I'm sorry about this morning. But I had to meet Myra. She was waiting for me."

Cate stood up and snatched her black and white Balenciaga bag off the couch. "You didn't have to do anything," she blurted out. Her deep blue eyes were wet. "I can't hear another word about you being BFFs with Myra Granberry." As she said the name, she made little quote signs in the air. "I have to go to Frédéric Fekkai to get my hair done, then I have to finish stuffing these gift bags, then hang that banner. That way when Blythe, Priya, and Sophie arrive, it'll at least *seem* like I have friends." Cate threw her bag over her shoulder and darted into the foyer, her Theory platform slides making a clacking sound against the marble floor.

"Cate!" Stella called, just as she heard the door slam. "You *do* have friends." But she knew the truth. She'd ignored Cate's text yesterday about Myra's makeover, and while she was at Bliss, watching Myra squirm in her chair as the woman tickled her feet with a pumice stone, Cate was stuffing five boxes of cupcakes into a cab. Tonight was Cate's chance to show the Beta Sigma

Phis her brilliant new friends, but Stella and Myra had formed a two-person faction without her.

Stella climbed onto the credenza, clutching the banner in her hand. Maybe she *had* been MIA for the last twenty-four hours. Maybe she *hadn't* helped Cate decide if they should get pink M&M's or purple. But it didn't matter. When the new Myra showed up in her Diane von Furstenberg dress, the three of them would have a dance party in the living room, or sit around the kitchen table laughing about the five-page petition Paige Mortimer e-mailed to Cate explaining, again, why she should be the third member. Betsy Carmichael would snap a million pictures of them for the *Ashton News* website, and by the end of the party Cate would find Myra's "goshes" and "gollies" so endearing she'd want to buy a pair of rainbow knee-highs of her own. By the end of the night everyone—including Cate—would finally see Chi Sigma Mu for what it was: the best sorority at Ashton Prep.

GUNTHER GUNTA: MAN. MYTH. COMPLETE MANIAC.

Lola poured the last drop of oil onto her head, watching as it disappeared into her scalp. She'd run around the house all morning, trying to find something, anything, that would help her look "one with the guttaaa." She finally settled on a bottle of olive oil, working it into her roots.

"What do you think, Heathy?" The giant tabby cat was curled up on the polka-dotted bath mat in the corner. He opened his eyes. "I know," Lola answered, staring at her reflection in the bathroom mirror. "I'm still not dirty enough." Her hair had taken on a greenish tint and the roots were so greasy they stuck up an inch off her scalp. But her skin still looked freshly washed, and she didn't have the same gutter stink she had yesterday. The shoot was in an hour. She needed to figure something out—immediately.

She darted up the stairs to her mum's room. Emma had a whole drawer of cosmetics, mostly complimentary gift baskets from MAC, Bobbi Brown, and Dior. With some bronzer under her eyes and a little gray eye shadow "dirt" here or there, Gunther would think she'd spent the last two days in a petting zoo.

Lola paused in the doorway of the loo, watching as her grandmother contorted her body like a circus performer, trying to cover the liver spots on her back with foundation. "Lola!" she hooted, jumping in surprise. She adjusted the straps of her red halter dress. "You gave me quite a fright! Be a dear and cover that spot on my back for me? I want Walter to think 'sixty-eight and sexy,' not 'sixty-eight and spotted.'"

Lola took the makeup sponge from her hand. "Grandmum," she said, blotting the foundation over a dark brown spot that was shaped a little like Africa. Margot smiled at her reflection in the mirror, tousling her stiff blond hair. "I took a shower. . . ."

"Oh, luv! I knew something was different. There isn't that rubbish stench lingering in the air." Margot kept her eyes on her reflection, pushing her pea-size hearing aid farther into the cave of her ear.

Lola pulled open her mom's makeup drawer, rifling through a pile of eye shadows in fifteen different shades of purple. "But Grandmum." She opened another drawer, searching for the bronzer. "Gunther is going to be gutted. I'm supposed to go to the shoot soon."

"Nonsense," Margot said, spinning around. She turned the bottle of MAC foundation onto the sponge wedge. "I can make you gutter chic." With that, Margot worked at Lola's face, pressing the walnut colored foundation into the hollows of her cheeks. She dabbed it below her eyes, making it look like Lola hadn't slept in days. "I met Gunther back in '88 in Belgium," she hummed, as Lola watched her reflection transform into a greasy, dirty mess. "His glasses are so thick he'll never know the difference."

An hour later, Lola stood outside a warehouse on Canal Street, staring at her reflection in her Hello Kitty compact. After dabbing foundation all over her face, her grandmum had put bronzer on her cheeks and over her nails, completing her dirty, urban look. Then, on her way downtown Lola splashed in a few sewer puddles to get back the gutter stench she had yesterday. She even wore her Gap hoodie from dinner, which still smelled faintly of curdled milk. She was as "one with the guttaaa" as a subway rat.

She smoothed back her oily blond hair. When she entered the shoot Gunther would circle her, pulling his thick glasses down to the end of his nose. *Yes, you aaahhh my guttaaa and my light!* He'd smile, delighted as he took in Lola's greasy hair and brown caked fingernails. She'd pose in his couture evening gown while he snapped photos of her clutching a loaf of stale bread. *Purfaction!* he'd scream, as she turned sideways to show off her ears. *Puuurfaction!*

Inside, a forest green garbage truck was parked in the center of the warehouse. It was surrounded by mounds of black bags and a tattered stuffed bear was strapped to its grill. Men in sweaty black T-shirts ran back and forth, setting crushed Coke cans and crumpled newspapers down on the floor, or adjusting the lighting. Lola clapped her hands together, small and fast. She'd been to a million photo shoots before with her mum, but none this exciting. Because this time, *she* was the model.

In the far corner of the room, Gunther stood next to a long catering table covered with miniature sandwiches. He downed a wheatgrass shot with one quick gulp. "And dat ez why you do ze good deeds—ze karma, Evette!" he said, wiping his mouth with the back of his hand. "Ze karma!" Evette studied her manicure, seemingly oblivious to Gunther's lecture.

Lola let out a deep breath, staring at the round little man who was about to change her life. She thought about the time Martin Cromwell told all the sixth-years she was anorexic, the time the rag mags put a picture of her picking her wedgie on the web, or the time she overheard her father whispering to her mum in the kitchen, wondering if "she'd grow into it." It was all in the past. From now on she was Lola Childs: Supermodel.

She ran toward him, her arms outstretched for a hug. "Gunther!" she cried.

"You ahhh feeelthy!" Gunther jumped backwards as he spotted her. Lola grabbed his wrist but he shook her off like she was some rabid animal. "Wat did you do?" He frantically searched the pockets of his white trousers, pulling out a small bottle of hand sanitizer. He poured it all over his arms, rubbing it in like it was suntan lotion.

Lola's cheeks felt hot. "You told me to be one with the gutter," she cried, looking from Gunther to Evette. "You said no bathing."

"He just meant he didn't want you to shower. You look like you've been sleeping in the subway station for the last week." Evette grabbed some Lysol from under the catering table and sprayed it in the air around her.

"You smeeell like ze poo-poo!" Gunther paced back and forth, muttering furiously. "I can't do zeees. She ez feelthy. Ze hair ez greasy oil." He smoothed back his thick black hair, took three wheatgrass shots off the catering table, and downed them one after the next.

"I'm sorry . . ." Lola mumbled. "Please. I can wash my hair."

"No!" Gunther screamed, his eyes wide behind his thick glasses. "It ez too late—everyone eez here." He gestured to the other end of the warehouse, where the lighting crew was standing, watching him flail his arms in frustration. A man wearing headphones subtly snapped a picture with his iPhone.

"I'm sorry," Lola repeated, feeling a lump in the back of her throat. She never should've taken that shower, or poured olive oil all over her hair. Now she'd have to go back to the town house—the party—and explain to everyone why she'd been fired by one of the greatest fashion designers in the world. Cate would tell the story at every Christmas dinner from now on, laughing as she described Lola's greasy hair. As soon as her mum came home from Tahiti, Ayana would ring her, specifically requesting Lola never set foot in the Ford building again. It was bad enough she'd embarrassed herself—she didn't need her mum knowing what a twit she'd been.

Gunther's eyes were bulgy, watery, and red. He squatted on the floor, his face a deep pink. "I am not ze maniac, I am not ze maniac," he muttered quietly, to no one in particular. "Evette—my bag!" Evette pulled a paper lunch bag out of her red leather purse. *Gunther* was scribbled in Sharpie across the front of it. He kept his eyes on the floor as he breathed in and out, filling it up like a balloon.

After a few more breaths Gunther set the bag down, his cheeks bright red. "It ez ze universe, Evette! It ez ze universe teeeesting me! Universe say: Gunther, you still ze maniac? I say no." Gunther stood up, adjusting his thick glasses. There was a new calm over his face as he pounded his little fist in the air. "We will do ze shoot!"

Evette's gaze fell on Lola's hands. They were caked in bronzer, like she'd been clawing her way through dirt. "Are you sure?"

"Yes." Gunther covered his heart with his hand. "Rodrrrrigo!" he called across the warehouse. A man with a handlebar mustache stood up. "Get ze dress!"

Lola let out a deep breath. Maybe she *was* "feeelthy." Maybe she *hadn't* followed Gunther's orders exactly. But Gunther saw something in her, and whatever that something was, she'd show it to him again. When he saw her pose . . . he'd be thrilled.

Fifteen minutes later, Lola emerged from the curtained-off section of the warehouse used as a dressing room. The makeup artist had tried to remove as much of the foundation as possible while Rodrigo, the stylist, fitted her in the first of four original Gunther Gunta evening gowns. The gray "gutter-inspired" dress was spotted with brown paint, as though she'd trudged through a muddy field. "I love it," Lola cried, spinning around once. Even with her hair greased up with olive oil, even with bronzer caked under her fingernails, she'd never felt so beautiful. She was a model now—a model for *Gunther Gunta*.

"It's actually not bad," Evette decided, puffing on a cigarette as she looked Lola up and down. "It's very '90s grunge—don't you think?"

Gunther was standing by the garbage trucks, his short arms folded over his chest. "I am not going for ze '90s grunge, Evette." He gestured for Lola to stand by the garbage truck and picked up his Nikon camera.

Lola stared at her reflection in the lens. She'd watched so many shoots and runway shows growing up that she had all of her mum's moves memorized—the way she turned and rested her chin on her shoulder, the way she put her hand on the back of her neck and stared directly into the camera. She went through each one, slowly, carefully, as Gunther clicked away.

Gunther let out a low growl, the same sound Heath Bar made whenever Cate walked in the room. Lola kept posing, trying to ignore it, but it kept getting louder. She rested a foot on a mound of garbage bags, which felt like they were stuffed with newspaper. When she tossed her oily hair over her shoulder, it stuck to the side of her face. She shook her head to get it off and a strand of hair got stuck in her mouth. It tasted like olive oil.

"Arrrgh," Gunther finally cried, throwing the camera onto the concrete floor. The lens broke off, rolling toward the door. He pulled at his hair and stomped his right foot several times. Lola stepped back, afraid. "I cannot do zeees. It ez crepe, Evette, crepe!" With that, he stormed out of the warehouse, slamming the door behind him.

"Crepe?" Lola asked, glancing around the room. The crew had all turned to watch. By the catering table in the corner, Rodrigo held a bagel to his mouth, frozen.

"Crap, Lola." Evette dropped her cigarette on the floor and stomped it out with her foot. Her black eyes narrowed. "He thinks you're crap."

Lola's eyes swelled with tears. She'd been so dim. Last night she'd talked to Abby online for an hour, keeping on about how Gunther had told her she was "freeeesh looking," or how Kyle would be barmy when he saw her billboard in Times Square. This wasn't her chance to be a supermodel, it was her chance to do the same thing she always did: act like a silly, awkward twit.

SOME GUYS GET ALL THE GIRLS

Saturday evening Stella stood in her closet, trying to decide on an outfit for the party. After Cate returned from her haircut she'd stormed up to her room. Stella intercepted her in the stairwell but she'd insisted she didn't want to talk about Myra, or the party planning, or anything anymore. She'd said she wanted "to have fun tonight." But as Cate closed her door in Stella's face, she couldn't help feeling like whatever "fun" Cate had, it wouldn't include her.

She walked her fingers over her clothes, finally pulling an Anna Sui dress from the hanger. She tugged hard, but the skirt was caught on something. Stella felt the wall, freeing the hem from behind a small rusty latch. She pushed the clothes aside, revealing a door of some sort. But it was sealed off with paint.

Stella knelt down and examined the small trapdoor. It reminded her of that story her father used to read to her and Lola when they were little—about Narnia, and the kids who went to another world through a passage in their wardrobe. After that they'd spent every afternoon in the hall closet, wearing their mum's old fur coats and pretending they were exploring a winter wonderland filled with talking badgers and magical fauns. Stella stuck her fingernail in the groove of the door frame, breaking the seal. As she ran her finger all along the edge, chips of green paint fell to the floor like confetti. She leaned against the door, but it was stuck.

She imagined a dusty stone passageway leading to paradise. Maybe a yacht on the French Riviera, or the pebble beach in Positano her grandmum took her to every summer. If nothing else, maybe she'd have room to expand her walk-in closet. She pushed hard against it once, then again, and finally there was a ripping sound. Then she fell face-first onto a wood floor. She looked up and saw . . . a fit bloke in plaid pajama pants. He was standing in the middle of the room, his hair sticking up in different directions, like he'd just rolled out of bed. Forget the French Riviera—*this* was paradise.

"Hi . . ." he said. Then he glanced behind Stella, where strips of flowery wallpaper hung over a gaping square hole. "We have a front door, you know." He let out a little laugh, squeezing the orange and blue Nerf basketball clutched in his hand.

"I'm sorry," Stella said quickly, brushing plaster snowflakes off her dress. The room was bare except for a four-poster bed and a stack of cardboard boxes in the corner. "I found this door in my closet and thought it was a secret passage or something."

"I hated that wallpaper anyway." He peered into the hole. "And technically it *is* a secret passage . . . to my bedroom." He smiled, then sank the ball into a small net perched above his window.

The word *bedroom* hung in the air between them. Stella felt like her stomach was filled with moths. This boy was cute and funny, and from now on the only thing that would separate them, night after night, was an unlocked door. She stepped forward and stuck out her hand. "I'm Stella Childs."

The boy took it in his own. "I'm Eli Punch." Stella stared at their hands, clasped together, feeling the heat creep into her cheeks. So this was the mysterious Eli Punch. The neighbor from Westport, Connecticut, with the father who'd played basketball for the Clippers. The connoisseur of chocolate pudding. No wonder Cate was obsessed with him. "You're Cate's sister?"

"*Stepsister,*" Stella corrected, finally letting go. "From London. I just moved here."

"Me too." Eli picked up the ball again and slam-dunked it in the net. "Is the Upper East Side all you hoped for and more?" He smirked.

Stella heard the question but didn't bother answering it. Her gaze had settled behind Eli, where a framed poster was resting against the wall. "Magritte," she said, as if she'd just recognized an old friend standing in the middle of Eli's bedroom. The painting was called *The Empire of Light, II,* and it had been her favorite, ever since she'd visited New York last fall and seen it hanging in the MoMA.

"Yeah," Eli said. "You like him?"

"I love him." She walked over and rested her fingers on the glass. The picture was of a street in darkness, but the sky behind it was bright. "It's brilliant, the way it's day and night at the same time." When Stella walked around New York on a nice day, she sometimes imagined she was in a Magritte painting. The sky in London was often gray, but here it was a clear blue, with perfect white clouds that looked like spoonfuls of marshmallow fluff.

"I'm obsessed with art." Eli smiled. He squeezed behind the cardboard boxes and slid out two other framed posters. "I'm just terrible at it."

"Rothko," Stella said, pointing at an abstract painting with orange and red rectangles. "And Kandinsky." Stella had painted a smaller version of *Squares with Concentric Rings* for her art class at Sherwood Academy, when they were learning how to do reproductions. She'd given it to her dad before they left for New York, even though she and he both knew, without saying, that he didn't deserve it.

Eli rested his hand against the wall, leaning in so that his face was close to Stella's. "How do you know so much about art?"

"I paint, and draw. . . ." Stella trailed off, noticing the foot of space between them. She hadn't been that close to a boy since Pippa's New Year's Eve party last year. She'd snogged Henry Cunningham on her roof deck, Big Ben just visible in the distance.

"You should show me your work sometime." Eli rapped his knuckles on the glass frame.

Stella smiled. Eli Punch could sink a basket from across the room *and* he knew who René Magritte was. "I will."

She glanced at her Movado watch. She could've stayed in Eli's room all night, keeping on about the John Currin exhibit she'd seen at the Whitney, and how she loved *The Scream*, even though she got the chills every time she looked into the creepy ghost man's eyes. But the party was starting in less than an hour and she was still unshowered, wearing her Topshop sweatpants and a T-shirt. "I better go."

"I'll see you tonight?" Eli asked. "I'm coming to the party."

"Of course." Stella ducked through the small door and glanced back at him, noticing for the first time how big his smile was. "And from now on . . . you know where to find me."

She closed the door behind her and fell against it. Ever since they'd moved in, she'd hated her room. She hated that she had to climb four flights of stairs to get to it. She hated that the ceilings were slanted and she had to duck so she didn't hit her head. But she was starting to think it was the best room in the house.

A PICTURE'S WORTH A THOUSAND WORDS

Andie walked around the living room with Clay, feeling like she was in a mosh pit. The party had started less than an hour ago, but already the town house was packed with ninth-graders from Haverford and Ashton Prep, and it seemed like every other person was clutching one of those silly Polaroid cameras. Cindy and Lola were sitting under the Chi Sigma Mu banner. Lola was still miserable from the failed shoot, but every once in a while she snapped a candid of Cindy blowing her nose. A brace-faced couple made out on the couch, completely oblivious to the three Haverford boys taking pictures of them.

Andie stood back as two ninth-grade boys wrestled on the floor, grinding personalized Chi Sigma Mu chocolates into the Persian rug. They rolled over, trapping Andie and Clay in the corner.

"I got you," Clay said. And without another word he picked Andie up and set her down on the other side of the rug. Then he hurdled over the boys.

"Thanks," Andie said, rubbing her hips where Clay had held her. Even if he'd already given two wedgies (one to Jake Goldfarb and one to Austin Thorpe's younger brother, Corey), he looked objectively cute in his plaid green Urban Outfitters button-down . . . and Andie wasn't the only one who'd noticed. Paige Mortimer had talked her ear off about how Clay was such a "catch," even begging her to set her up with his older brother Jackson. Everyone was obsessed with Clay, and Andie couldn't help but be just the *tiniest* bit excited by all the attention.

"Photo op!" Shelley DeWitt called, shoving a Polaroid camera in Clay and Andie's face. Clay grabbed Andie's shoulder, pulling her so close her nose was buried in his armpit. "We need one of you two!"

Andie shielded her face with her hand. "I'm not feeling very . . . *photogenic.*" She peered through her fingers at the corkboard on the wall, which was covered in pictures. There was a glamour shot of Blythe, Priya, and Sophie pouting their lips, *Beta Sigma Phi* scrawled in the space below with purple Sharpie. There was another of Austin Thorpe's bare butt, on which someone had drawn eyes and a nose and written *Buttface Thorpe.* Andie imagined a picture labeled *Andie <3's Clay,* her cheek snuggled into the crook of Clay's arm. Even if Paige Mortimer and Shelley DeWitt were impressed with her new "boyfriend," there was one person who wouldn't be: Kyle Lewis. He'd be there in an hour, and she couldn't have photographic evidence of her fake relationship pinned up for everyone to see.

"Come on, Sloane," Clay said, squeezing her shoulder so hard it burned. But Shelley was already gone, darting across the room to snap a picture of the Ashton drama club jumping up and down by the fireplace, wailing "La Vie Bohème."

As they strolled into the foyer, Andie spotted Blythe. She was leaning against the wall with Priya and Sophie, and they were all wearing Alice + Olivia V-neck shirts in the three primary colors. She'd spent three years wishing they'd be friends with her. She couldn't just walk by without showing off her new boyfriend (even if he was fake). "Hey, guys," Andie cooed. "You know Clay Calhoun, right?"

Blythe grabbed Andie's arm. "You're not *dating* him—are you?" she whispered.

"Yes, I am," Andie bragged. Technically, she *was* dating him . . . at least until nine thirty. In forty-five minutes Clay would leave, and in an hour Kyle would arrive. They could hide out in her dad's study. Kyle would strum Winston's old Larrivée guitar from the '70s, away from the wall of Polaroid pictures, away from Clay Calhoun's personal fan club, and away from Lola.

Sophie bounced on her heels, as if she just realized who Clay Calhoun was. "O M to the G! Your mother plays Dr. Chartreuse Delacorte on that soap, *Saving Love!*"

Clay glanced at his Nike sneakers, his shaggy hair falling in his face. "Something like that."

"Hey, everyone!" a voice called. Danny Plimpton, a usually shy seventh-grader from Haverford, stood at the top of the stairs and waved. He was wearing dress pants and a shirt and tie, even though almost everyone was in jeans. Lola and Cindy hovered in the living room doorway to watch. "Look!" Three camera flashes went off as he slid down the polished mahogany banister and crashed into Betsy Carmichael. Her punch went flying through the air.

The marble foyer echoed with laughter. Paige Mortimer doubled over like she was about to pee her cropped Theory pants. Cate had just walked in wearing a sequined Phillip Lim minidress, her dark brown hair swept up, her mouth open in shock as she spotted the bright red tidal wave dripping down the ivory wall. "It's not funny," she cried, her hands balled into fists. "Someone's going to have to clean that up."

Andie watched as Cate pulled Danny aside by the ear. It seemed strange that Danny had come to the party at all, and even stranger that Cate knew who he was. But she'd dragged him into the kitchen and was now explaining the difference between "good attention" and "bad attention."

"You keeping on all right?" Lola asked, moving behind Clay and winking at Andie so much it looked like she was having an eye spasm. Her face still looked puffy and red from the Gunther shoot. Right before the party, Andie had discovered her crying in the bathroom. Her head was in the sink and she was scrubbing furiously, trying to get the olive oil out of her hair. Andie felt partially responsible. She'd given Lola the once-over before she left for the shoot. She *did* look dirty, and her hair *did* look like she'd styled it with a stick of butter, but she'd also insisted that was what Gunther had asked for.

"Clay's the best," Andie said. She leaned her head on his shoulder. But when she turned back at Lola, she was looking through her Polaroid camera, the lens leveled right at them. "No," Andie cried, as Lola's finger pushed down on the button. She was ready . . . she aimed . . . and she fired.

Andie tried to block it with her hand, but the flash blinded her. A photo shot out of the front of the camera. "Now we can put it on the wall," Lola said, shaking it back and forth.

"No!" Andie snatched the photo from Lola's hands. She could just make out the picture. She was standing next to Clay, her mouth open like she was mid-scream. One hand was reaching toward the camera. "I'll put this up later."

Lola glanced at it. "It's horrid, though. Let's take one more." She raised the camera again. That was it. Andie couldn't have the picture—or Lola—floating around the party anymore. It was too much of a liability, like having Hannah Marcus, who was infamously unathletic, on your intramural softball team. "Cindy? Don't you need some cough syrup or something?" She leveled her brown eyes at her friend.

"Rught. I do." Cindy's voice sounded like she was underwater. "Lola—cun you hulp me fund some?" She shot Andie a knowing look as she pulled Lola toward the staircase.

"Well, all right," Lola said, following her up the stairs.

"Do you huve uny of thugh Hurry Putter movies?" Cindy added, her gold bowler hat sitting askew on her head. "I thunk I may need to lie down fur uh-while . . ."

"Of course." Lola perked up. "Follow me." Cindy and Lola headed up the stairs, weaving through the Haverford freshmen who were now lined up, waiting to slide down the banister. Andie watched them disappear and let out a deep breath. She didn't care what Lola and Cindy were doing—watching a Harry Potter marathon, taking more Polaroids of each other, or giving Heath Bar a flea bath—the most important thing was that they were doing it on the third floor. As long as Lola and that annoying camera stayed there, she'd never know Kyle had ever shown up.

SECRETS, SECRETS ARE NO FUN . . .
SECRETS, SECRETS HURT SOMEONE

The party had been going on for over an hour, and there was still no sign of Myra. Stella wandered around the living room, hoping against hope she was hiding somewhere in all the chaos. By the fireplace, two Haverford boys roasted marshmallows on the wrought iron poker. An Ashton girl had grabbed Heath Bar and was attempting to feed him M&M's, his green eyes wide with fear. "I heard Myra looks like Claire Danes," the girl called out as she spotted Stella in the crowd.

Stella wrung her hands. "Right!" she yelled. "You'll see soon enough!" All night, people had been asking for Myra Granberry by name. Betsy Carmichael had posted an item about Myra on the *Ashton News* website that morning, encouraging people to come forward with any preliminary Myra sightings around the city. Paige Mortimer had set aside a whole packet of Polaroid film just for Myra's big reveal, and some of the Haverford blokes had even asked for Myra's phone number, sight unseen. It seemed like everyone was obsessed with *Extreme Makeover: Myra Granberry Edition.*

Stella had been texting Myra for the last hour, but hadn't gotten a reply. It wasn't like her not to respond. Stella was starting to worry something had happened. Maybe Myra had had an allergic reaction to her Armani Code perfume, or maybe she'd tripped in her new Manolos and was lying somewhere on Madison Avenue, her ankle twisted and swollen. Or maybe Pythagoras had gotten sick and she'd had to rush him to the veterinary clinic. Right now, anything seemed like a possibility.

"Stella!" Cate called from the doorway. "A word!" Then she walked over to the couch, where Blythe was snuggled with Sophie and Priya. "I hope you're taking notes on how to throw a party. I know it's hard for you to do anything without seeing my example first."

Blythe rolled her eyes. "I stopped taking notes after the page titled 'How to Lose Friends and Alienate People.'" Priya let out a little laugh, her nose ring sparkling in the light.

Cate pulled Stella into the foyer. She yanked so hard that Stella was afraid she'd dislocated her shoulder. "Everyone's asking where Myra is. What am I supposed to say?"

"I told you. She'll be here." Stella tried to sound calm, but it was almost nine. Stella had told Myra to be there at seven thirty—half an hour before all the guests came. She'd wanted her to come down the stairs for her big reveal, cheered on by the crowd gathered in the foyer. She'd even planned on Myra passing out the Polaroid cameras, so she could get to know the guests by name. But Myra had missed all of it. If she didn't show up soon, Stella would have to march over to her town house and escort her herself.

Cate dug her fingers into her palms. "You said that a half hour ago." She glanced into the living room where Blythe, Priya, and Sophie were now dancing to the Pussycat Dolls. Blythe popped her shoulders in and out. Priya laughed as Sophie shook uncontrollably, like there was electricity pulsing through her tiny body. Cate couldn't help thinking that if Stella had never wormed her way into the Chi Beta Phis, right now Cate would've been with them, twirling and dipping Priya so she didn't feel so self-conscious on the dance floor. Instead, she was waiting around for *Myra Granberry,* along with everyone else—and her reputation depended on it. "This is humiliating. Do you see that banner?" She pointed at the sign in the living room that read Chi Sigma *Mu.*

"Right." Stella nodded. "We need the Mu. I'll text her again."

"Good. Now I have to get the garden ready for my date with Eli." Cate turned on her heel, gently pressing down her messy bun to make sure it was still in place. Stella swallowed hard, but her mouth felt like it was filled with sand. She hadn't told Cate about the door yet—but right now that was the least of her problems. She whipped out her iPhone and texted furiously.

STELLA: WHERE R U?

Just then Betsy Carmichael grabbed Stella's arm. Her pink Diane von Furstenberg wrap dress was spotted with red punch. "Where's the Slug?" Her green eyes bulged from her head, making her look like an Amazon tree frog.

Stella gritted her teeth. "Her name is Myra," she snapped. "Not

Slug, not Sluggie, not Mug, or Mugsy, or the traditional Mug the Slug. Its just Myra—at least to you."

Betsy backed away, like she was afraid Stella might beat her over the head with her iPhone. Stella couldn't help it. She was so tired of everyone treating Myra like a bearded lady or a circus midget—just there for everyone's amusement. She couldn't wait for Myra to walk through the door and shut them up, once and for all. Her iPhone buzzed.

MYRA: I'M IN FRONT OF UR HOUSE

Stella darted outside. "Myra! I was so worried—" The heavy front door closed behind her, knocking her onto the steps. Standing outside the wrought iron gate was Myra . . . but not the Myra Stella was expecting. Her blond hair looked flat and stringy against her cheeks, and she was wearing her Mathletes T-shirt with neon green track pants. Her L.L. Bean backpack was high on her shoulders, making her look hunchbacked.

Stella took a deep breath, trying not to panic. She'd given Myra nearly two hours to get ready for the party, but it was as though she'd traveled back in time to three days ago. Nothing had changed. When Cate saw her she was going to hyperventilate. "What happened? You were supposed to be here an hour and a half ago." Myra gripped the fence, her knuckles turning white. The light from the foyer window fell on her face and Stella noticed her brown eyes were puffy and red. "What's wrong?"

Myra glared at Stella. "So I finally know why you've been so nice to me."

"What are you talking about?" Stella felt a bubbling in the pit of her stomach. Something wasn't right. The light from the window darkened, and Stella turned to see a few Ashton girls pressed against the glass.

"I know about your stupid challenge!" Myra yelled. Tears fell down her cheeks and she wiped them away with the back of her hands. "After I left you I saw Blythe Finley on Third Avenue. I walked behind her for three blocks, listening to her tell Priya Singh how ridiculous it was that you'd actually made me over. She just couldn't believe you took her seriously when she told you 'Mug the Slug' couldn't be the third member of Chi Sigma."

Stella's knees shook, her legs feeling like they might give out beneath her. "No. It wasn't like that," she managed. She'd nearly forgotten about Blythe's challenge. It felt like it had happened so long ago. Yes, it was technically the reason she'd wanted Myra as their third member, but things were different now—*she* was different.

"Then tell me. What *was* it like? Did you agree to make me over on a dare or not?" Myra crossed her arms over her chest. The window was full of people now, all pressed together in a tight row. A few banged on the glass to get their attention, like Stella and Myra were two monkeys at the zoo.

"Myra, I think—" Stella reached out for Myra's arm, but the other girl pulled away. A boy inside started chanting *Mug the Slug! Mug the Slug!* and Stella cringed as a camera flash went off.

Myra took a step back. "Yes or no?" She bit her bottom lip so hard it looked like it might bleed.

There was only one answer to the question. Stella stared

down at her red Marc Jacobs pumps, wishing she could click the heels together like Dorothy and go somewhere else—anyplace but here. "Maybe it started that way, but . . ."

Myra tucked her stringy hair behind her ears. "I can't believe how selfish you are. You and Cate must've had a great time, watching me get my lip waxed and parading me around in Diane von Fusterbutt dresses. Just do me a favor—next time you need some cheap entertainment, watch *The Hills*."

The front door opened a crack and Cate peeked her head outside. "I heard she's here." Cate froze when she noticed Myra. "Oh, no. What are those?" She hissed, pointing at the neon green track pants.

But Myra wasn't listening. She pulled her new Marc Jacobs bag out of her L.L. Bean backpack. "I won't be needing this any-more," she said, thrusting it into Stella's arms. Then she took off down Eighty-second Street.

"Where does she think she's going?" Cate stood next to Stella, her brows furrowed.

"Home." Stella stared down at the embossed *M.G.*, blinking back tears. She'd been so daft. She'd brought Myra to the Red Door Salon, to Saks, to Bliss, treating her like she was some poor child from the Make-a-Wish Foundation. She'd even felt proud of herself for helping Myra—for showing her that green shadow complemented her eye color, or that wrap dresses looked best on her petite frame—when it didn't mean a thing—any of it. Once again, Myra was right. Stella had been selfish, and condescending, and just as mean as every other girl at Ashton Prep. "She quit."

"What do you mean, '*She quit*'?" Cate growled. "I trusted you to make this work. She's our Mu." Cate bit down hard on her thumbnail. She'd just bragged to Kirsten Phillips about how spectacular Myra's new haircut looked, and spread a rumor through Shelley DeWitt that Myra's dad owned Belvedere Castle in Central Park. She'd even scanned Myra's eighth-grade yearbook picture for *Ashton News*, just to be certain Betsy would feature the before/after shots during Monday's homeroom. She couldn't go back into the party without Mug. Not now, and especially not with Blythe, Priya, and Sophie in there. Everyone would see her for who she was: a Beta Sigma Phi reject.

Stella sniffed back tears. She had enough to feel guilty about already, without Cate reminding her of her promise. They could cut the *Mu* off the banner, throw away the rest of the personalized chocolates, or they'd just tell people Myra had a headache and had to go home. It didn't matter what they said now—it mattered what they'd done these last two days. Stella had made Myra feel like a science experiment, the silly product of some silly, mean bet. "You know, there are more important things than bloody sororities," she spat. Then she went back inside, letting the door slam behind her.

TO: Abby Powell
FROM: Lola Childs
DATE: Saturday, 9:16 p.m.
SUBJECT: Ugh.

I know it's almost two in the morning there, and you're probably sleeping. But I needed someone to talk to.

The Gunther shoot was bad, Abby. Bad isn't even the word—it was horrid, worse than the time I fell on stage at fifth-grade awards night. I feel like such a bloody twit, as always. Gunther hates me, and my hair still looks like I haven't washed it in a week.

I wish I could be at your flat right now, eating ham-and-butter sandwiches in your kitchen. Instead I'm in my mum's room watching *Harry Potter* for the millionth time, alone. Or at least kind of alone. Andie's with her new boyfriend downstairs, so I promised her I'd keep an eye on Cindy, her best mate. But Cindy drank so much cough syrup she fell asleep on the bed twenty minutes ago. And Kyle's a no-show. I think he's politely telling me to bugger off.

I just miss you, and I want my mum to be back from her honeymoon already. And now Stella's in her room and won't answer her door.

Ring me tomorrow? Please?

Love,
Lola

IT WAS ONLY A KISS

"So then Brandon slipped and totally wiped out," Clay said, running a hand through his shaggy blond hair. "Puke everywhere." He reached over Andie and punched Brandon in the arm. Brandon laughed, exposing a row of green braces. His black hair was gelled in the front, forming stiff spikes.

"That's funny," Andie mumbled. She was trapped between them on the love seat in the den, listening to another one of Clay's stupid stories. This time it was about Brandon falling into a puke puddle on the 6 train. Andie glanced at the grandfather clock in the corner. It was nine twenty. Which meant in just ten minutes Clay and Brandon would be off to the Ludacris concert, and Andie would finally be free.

On the sofa Parker Adams was making out with her Haverford boyfriend, while two other couples faced off in foosball. Shelley DeWitt was perched in the window seat with Fillmore Weitz, whose skin looked surprisingly clear compared to the last time Andie had seen him. Everyone was paired off—everyone except

Andie. She was supposed to be Clay's girlfriend (even if it *was* fake), but ever since Brandon arrived she'd felt like a third wheel. A third wheel on an annoying, fist-pounding tricycle to Dude Land.

Just then Lola strolled in, carrying Heath Bar in her arms. "Lola?" Andie tried to steady her voice. "Where's Cindy? I thought you guys were watching movies in dad's room?"

"I'm bloody bored. Cindy fell asleep twenty minutes ago." Lola looked around the den. "I can't watch the telly when everyone is down here having . . ." She trailed off, her gaze falling on Parker and her boyfriend. Parker was sucking on her boyfriend's ear. She was going to say *fun* but that didn't seem like *quite* the right word anymore. Parker made snogging look scary, like her tongue was in a boxing match with her boyfriend's ear.

"What's the deal with your hair?" Brandon asked.

"Nothing . . ." Lola smoothed down her headband, feeling her face flush. Since the shoot she'd washed it three times but it was still greasy. Even worse, it looked a little green, like it used to get in London, after she spent all day in Abby's indoor swimming pool. She'd spent so much time trying to become one with the gutter, she'd never considered how she'd get *out* of the gutter. All she had to show for her brush with supermodeling was a stringy mop of hair that smelled like her grandmother's olive grove in Tuscany.

"Maybe you should check on Cindy. She might need help." Andie's heart sped up. Kyle would be here any minute. If Lola was wandering around the house, she wouldn't be able to talk to him, or look at him, without feeling like she was under FBI surveillance.

"She's fine." Lola tugged on the bottom of her black, long-sleeved T-shirt. It was covered with an inch of orange fur.

"Then as soon as Clay leaves I'll go upstairs with you to wake Cindy up. I just don't want her"—Andie searched for an excuse—"sleeping on my dad's bed." Even if Cindy had snuck out of her house with a stuffy nose and a bad cough, she was only there because she promised to watch Lola. Cough syrup or no cough syrup, Andie needed her awake.

"Sleeping on the bed?" Lola furrowed her brows. "Mum and Winston won't care." She held Heath Bar over her shoulder and bounced him up and down like he was a twenty-pound, fur-covered newborn.

On the love seat, Clay and Brandon had started punching each other. They reached behind Andie and in front of her, trying to get at each other. "You're an idiot!" Clay hooted, standing to knock Brandon hard in the shoulder. Brandon pulled the hood of his orange Triple 5 Soul sweatshirt over his head and ducked behind Andie, using her as a shield.

Parker noticed Clay's clenched fist, which was pulled back like he was aiming for Andie. "What's your problem?" she yelled. "Isn't that your girlfriend?" Her red hair was staticky from making out, and it floated up on one side, as though she'd just rubbed a balloon to it.

"Yeah," Clay said. "I wasn't aiming for her—I was aiming for Brandon." He sat back down on the leather couch, wrapping an arm around Andie.

"Well maybe you should stop punching your friend and start making out," Parker said with a laugh, revealing two snaggleteeth that made her look just a little bit menacing, like a friendly vampire.

"Yeah," Parker's boyfriend hooted. His face was bright pink from making out, like he'd just come out of a sauna. "Get it on!"

Andie felt Clay's arm around her shoulder, like a cold, dead snake. This had gone too far. Clay wasn't actually her boyfriend, and she definitely didn't want to make out with him. He'd probably stick his fat tongue down her throat so far it would touch her tonsils. Besides, she wanted her first kiss to be with Kyle—lead singer of the Wormholes, snowboarding, soccer-playing, genuinely nice, silly Kyle. "Right." Andie laughed, pretending it was just a joke. She inched away from Clay and pulled her polka-dotted Milly blouse closer around her neck.

"Do it! Do it!" Brandon chanted. He glanced around the room for support. The couples playing foosball joined in, raising their arms and cheering. A boy in a vintage Dr Pepper T-shirt even stomped his foot, shaking the flat screen on the wall.

Clay leaned toward Andie, his lips pursed and his eyes closed in concentration. He was so close she could smell his Doritos breath. She didn't want to do this, she couldn't. But she could feel Lola watching her. She was chanting too, her lilting British accent making her voice stand out from all the rest.

Andie ran her hands along the top of her J Brand jeans. Maybe she could kiss Clay—just a peck. She closed her eyes, waiting for Clay's lips to touch down on hers. She could feel his breath getting closer and closer, the Cool Ranch smell stinging her nostrils.

Do it, do it, do it! echoed in her ears. Her whole body was tense, braced as though she were about to get hit by a baseball, flying ninety miles an hour at her face. She felt Clay's lips press against hers, their plumpness giving way. She held them there as the chant broke into hoots and cheers. Someone screamed, "Yee-ha!" When she pulled away, her face felt hot, like she had a hundred and one–degree fever.

Across the room, she felt someone's eyes on her. There, in the doorway, was Kyle Lewis. He looked like someone had just put his Fender guitar through a wood chipper. "You're early . . ." Andie mumbled.

"Kyle!" Lola called, clapping her hands together. "You came!" She bounded over to him, but Kyle stood frozen.

He looked at Andie, then Clay, then back at Andie, his hands clenched together in tight fists. "You're with *him*?" He was wearing a tattered Ramones T-shirt and dark blue jeans.

Andie's hands trembled. What was she supposed to say? *No, I was just pretending I'm Clay's boyfriend, because Lola likes you and would kill me if she knew I was dating you?* There was no way to explain it. She looked at Kyle, chewing the MAC lip gloss from her lips.

Kyle's brown eyes looked wet. "Here," he said, pushing past Lola to drop a CD case into Andie's lap. On the front of it was a picture of his band under the lights at Arlene's Grocery. Kyle was wearing his headband and aviators. "I made this for you—it's all the new songs you heard on Friday. Enjoy." When he said *enjoy,* it sounded more like, *Have a nice life.* With that, he stormed out.

Andie stared at the CD, feeling like Kyle had just tossed a bomb in her lap. She'd dated Ben Carter for a month last year.

Their entire relationship had consisted of passing notes back and forth in math class, until she got so bored she broke up with him. And even if everyone else liked Clay, she couldn't spend two hours with him without wishing she had earplugs. But everything with Kyle was different. She would've stayed up all night talking to him online, even if she got detention for falling asleep in first-period history. She would've gone to every one of his concerts for the next two years, just on the chance that he might've written a song about her—*for* her.

"Who's the toolbag?" Brandon asked, watching Kyle run down the stairs. His hiccupy laugh made Andie wince.

You're the toolbag, Andie thought as she inched away from him. Kyle didn't use the word *dude* in every other sentence, or have punching contests. And he could have a conversation about more than just soccer or pantsing his best friend. He was nothing like Brandon, or Clay, and that was a good thing. Maybe the best thing about him. She turned the CD over in her hands, sniffing back tears. Whether she thought that or not, Kyle didn't know. All he knew was that she was kissing Clay Calhoun, the guy who poured Gatorade over his head at the soccer scrimmage. She could forget being Kyle's girlfriend now—she'd be lucky if he ever talked to her again.

"Seriously, though, Sloane," Clay whispered. He pulled his arm from Andie's shoulders. "What's the deal with that kid?" For the first time ever, he looked worried.

"That's Kyle Lewis," Lola hissed. She squeezed Heath Bar so hard he let out a loud mew. Andie had gone to Kyle's band practice. Kyle Lewis. The same Kyle she'd walked along the Thames with as a child, watching the salmon jump. The same Kyle whom she'd watched play cricket at London Fields, even when it was raining. And the same Kyle she'd (just last week!) gone on a date with to Madame Tussauds. He was *her* Kyle. And Andie had been sneaking around behind her back, letting her keep on about how he'd been MIA. *Give him some time*, she'd said!

"You bloody liar," Lola muttered, her nose twitching. She had been right all along. Kyle *was* talking to someone else. But it wasn't Imaginary Girl, with her long silky blond hair and her tiny, perfect ears. It was *Andie*.

"No, Lola," Andie started, but Lola turned and ran up the stairs. Heath Bar looked over Lola's shoulder, shooting Andie a disapproving look.

The entire den was watching her. Parker Adams's jaw dropped open in a dramatic *O*. Andie let out a deep breath, wishing everyone would just go home. It was useless. Lola was convinced she was a lying, sneaky backstabber, and Kyle was convinced she was a cheating, boy-crazy idiot. And the worst part was, both of them were right.

THAT'S WHAT FRIENDS ARE FOR

Betsy Carmichael followed Cate to the kitchen, a tiny Kate Spade notebook perched in her hand. "Is Myra officially out of Chi Sigma Mu? *Ashton News* wants to know."

Cate wheeled around. Betsy had been trailing her through the party like some annoying gnat, constantly buzzing in her ear. *Did Myra leave for personal reasons? Why is Stella upstairs in her room? Overall, would you consider the Chi Sigma Mu mixer a success?* It took all of Cate's restraint not to smack her away. "This is the last time I'm going to tell you. No. Comment." Cate spat each word in Betsy's face. Betsy finally retreated to the living room, where a group of girls from the drama club were now singing along to Lady Gaga. They were using an expensive, delicate glass vase as a microphone, but Cate was too tired to care.

She trudged through the kitchen, the floor sticking to the bottom of her red Katia Lombardo heels. This was supposed to be *her* night. She and Stella were going to toast Myra in the living room and start a dance party on the couch. They were going to pose for Polaroids in the foyer and walk around together, arm in arm, so Cate could finally have new memories—ones that didn't include Blythe. Stella had promised Myra would be here, primped and primed and ready to be their number three. And Cate had trusted her. Now everything—the makeover, the party, Chi Sigma—felt like a huge mistake.

Cate stared at the Chi Sigma Mu cupcakes on the granite island, each one with three sugar Greek letters set in the icing. Danny Plimpton was hunched over the round cherry table, using pink and purple M&M's to play tic-tac-toe with himself. The poor boy had finally gotten up the nerve to approach Lola, only to discover she'd locked herself in her room. Besides him, the kitchen was empty.

Cate slowly picked the *Mu* off each cupcake, collecting them in her hand. Eli would be there any minute. She could handle the questions from Betsy, or how Paige Mortimer kept shooting her *I told you you should have picked me* looks. But Eli was the one person she refused to be embarrassed in front of. For tonight it was Chi Sigma—no Mu. She'd just pretend that had been the plan from the beginning.

"What are you doing?" a familiar voice said. Cate spun around to see Priya standing in the doorway, fingering her black curls. Blythe and Sophie followed her into the kitchen. Panicked, Cate shoved the whole handful of letters in her mouth. The sugary taste made her gag.

"I'm sorry about what happened with Myra," Blythe said.

Cate stared at her former best friend. This was the same Blythe she'd met in preschool, bonding over Tinkertoys. The same Blythe who went to the dentist with her when she had her first cavity, just because she knew how terrified Cate was of drills. But everything felt different now—uncertain. There Blythe was, standing in Cate's kitchen with Priya and Sophie, who just two weeks ago were following *her* around.

If Cate asked Blythe to let her back in to Chi Beta Phi, things could return to normal. They could all go upstairs to her room right now and sprawl out on her queen-size bed, the way they always did at sleepovers. She could tell them about the wedding, and how her dad had teared up when he'd recited his vows. And she could show them the old pictures she found in Winston's study—of her parents' cross-country road trip, and her mom's baby photos, and the one of her when she was nineteen, acting in the off-Broadway production of *Anything Goes*. Cate rubbed the sapphire ring on her finger. Even if she and Blythe weren't friends anymore, it sometimes felt like Blythe was the only person in the world who understood. Because she was the only person who had really been there.

Her ex-friends were standing together against the wall. Sophie was still humming quietly, barely able to look at her. Things would never be exactly the same as they were before. But nothing could be worse than this. Cate let out a deep breath. "I was thinking—"

"Just for the record, I didn't mean to tell Myra about the challenge," Blythe interrupted. "I didn't even know she was behind us."

Cate was wrong. Things *could* be worse. "*You're* the reason Myra stormed off?" She dug her fingernails into her palm. Of course Blythe had told Myra about the challenge. Blythe had always been terrified of real competition. She'd quit the track team the first time she lost a race.

"Cate," Blythe said, taking a step toward her, "it was an accident. But honestly, it's for the best. Myra Granberry? Come on. You're better than that." She pulled her shoulders back. "Come back to us. I'll let you into Beta Sigma Phi."

"Oh, you'll *let* me?" Cate stared into Blythe's gray eyes. As tempting as it was to think about having her friends back, she couldn't rejoin them as one of Blythe's sheep. It was just too degrading. "No, thanks," Cate said, standing up straighter. Even if Blythe had ruined Chi Sigma Mu, there was still one thing Cate had that she didn't. "Eli Punch is going to be here any minute." She let the words sink in. "We have a date."

"*What?*" Blythe's head jerked back, like Cate had just spit in her face.

Right then, Cate spotted Eli in the foyer, moving through the crowd. His J. Crew button-down was wrinkled, like he'd just rolled out of bed. "And here he is now . . ." Cate singsonged. She pushed past the Beta Sigma Phis as she left the kitchen. "Eli!"

"Hey." He glanced around the packed foyer. A Haverford boy in an Obama T-shirt jumped back, knocking Cate into Eli's chest. He looked down at her and smiled. "Your party is insane, Cate."

"Insane in a good way or a bad way?"

He peeked in the living room, where Paige Mortimer and her friend were dancing on Winston's leather club chair to the new Rihanna song. On the floor, a boy in a Haverford hoodie made a poor attempt at break dancing. "A good way." Eli laughed.

The Beta Sigma Phis were watching her from the kitchen

doorway. Suddenly everything—Myra's makeover, the fighting with Blythe, Chi Sigma Mu—didn't feel as important anymore. With Eli this close to her, it was easy to forget.

Cate pulled him into the kitchen, her eyes locking with Blythe's. "You know Eli, right?" She could relax a little now that her *date* had arrived. Once Eli was her boyfriend she would never be alone, no matter what Blythe said or did. She could forbid Priya and Sophie to look at her, she could pit Myra and Stella against each other, she could sabotage every third member they ever tried to induct. Once Eli was her boyfriend, she would always have someone to stand beside her at parties, or celebrate with her when she got called back for the second round of musical auditions.

"Hi," Blythe mumbled, glancing at her Juicy espadrilles. "We were actually just leaving. Right?" Blythe turned to Priya and Sophie.

"Yeah." Priya nodded. "We have another party we're late for." She grabbed Blythe's elbow and the two walked out, Sophie trailing close behind.

Eli's cheeks were bright red. "That was kind of . . . awkward." He scratched the back of his neck. "Do you think we can go talk somewhere—*privately*?" Danny Plimpton paused his game of tic-tac-toe and turned to Cate, mouthing something that looked like *The Eagle has landed.* Then he gave her the thumbs-up.

Cate smoothed back her dark brown hair, excited. "I know the perfect place." She pushed out the kitchen door. Before the party started, she'd spent a half hour in the garden, staging it for her and Eli's first kiss. Tea lights were scattered over every surface, making the space look like it was infested with fireflies. There were cupcakes and M&M's on the coffee table, and she'd set up her iPod and portable speakers in the upstairs window. The ivied backyard was now filled with the sounds of Vampire Weekend. Everything was perfect.

They sat down on the teak sofa, and Eli leaned back against the cushion. She hadn't hung out with a boy since Charlie. They'd met for two days while on vacation in Hawaii, but she'd always known he would go back to Minnesota, and she would go back to New York. It was easier with him, because there was a time limit. He could never *really* be her boyfriend. With Eli she worried she was talking too loud, the way she always did when she was nervous, or that bits of dinner were stuck in her teeth. There was an echo in her head, like she could hear herself saying every word to him, wondering if it sounded rehearsed, or just silly. Sometimes it was scary to like someone so much.

"I wasn't expecting to see Blythe here." Eli looked adorable in his pale blue J. Crew button-down, but his face was tense with worry.

"I know. She just showed up." Cate ran her hands along the hem of her Phillip Lim dress, the sequins feeling scratchy against her palms. "It was really weird." She shrugged, as if to say, *That's just the kind of sketchball she is.*

"You were right about Blythe." Eli sighed, pushing his thick black hair off his forehead.

Cate let out a deep breath. She'd known Eli would see through her. He belonged with someone who could pull an amazing outfit together (even at Marshalls), who was president of the Spanish Honor Society and the French Honor Society, who could play the lead in Annie while simultaneously organizing the eighth-grade formal at the Puck Building. He belonged with someone *loyal.* Someone like Cate.

"When we were at Jackson Hole she kept talking about her friends and how they're the most popular girls at Ashton Prep," Eli continued. "She's definitely not for me." He leaned in close and smiled.

Cate's stomach felt tight, like she'd just looked over the ledge of a forty-story building. All the humiliation she felt at the basketball game and the torture she'd endured imagining Blythe and Eli holding hands on a carriage ride through Central Park felt far away, like something that had happened when she was in fourth grade. Because now she was in her candlelit garden, alone with Eli, close enough that she could feel his breath on her face.

She leaned in just the tiniest bit and stared into Eli's dark eyes. *Just kiss me,* she thought, waiting for him to bring his lips to hers. But Eli looked through the window, his eyes searching the kitchen. "Is Stella here?" he asked.

"Stella?" Cate squeaked.

"Yeah." Eli smiled innocently, like the question was as benign as asking Cate to pass the M&M's.

"No . . ." Cate trailed off, falling back against the hard wooden slats of the teak sofa. Eli didn't seem to notice.

"What's her deal?" He lowered his voice, as if afraid someone was hiding in the bushes and might overhear. "Does she have a boyfriend?"

Cate could feel a baseball-size lump rising in the back of her throat. When—and how—had Stella and Eli met? She was dying to know, but didn't want to reveal that Stella hadn't told her about it. Instead, she managed, "Why do you want to know?" She already knew the answer. No one in the history of the world had asked that question unless they liked the person they were asking it about.

"I was just wondering . . ." Eli was still looking past Cate, inside the lit windows of the town house. "She just seems cool. Please don't mention that I asked, though."

Cate tried hard to smile, but her face felt stiff. She wasn't going to cry. She couldn't. Not in front of Eli. "I won't."

"Thanks." Eli squeezed her shoulder. "You're a good friend."

Cate turned away, cringing at that word. *Friend.* She knew everything about Eli—how he couldn't pass a dog on the street without petting it, how his mom had been born and raised in Tokyo, how he had a horrible case of mono last year that kept him out of school for a month. It was *his* turn to learn everything about *her.* She wanted him to know that she loved blue roses, even though they weren't real and were only sold at cheap delis along Third Avenue. She wanted him to ask her about the tiny scar on her knee, so she could tell the story of how she slipped climbing a waterfall in Samoa. He needed to know about her mom, and the cancer, and how she hated going anywhere—even into the shower—without wearing her blue sapphire ring, or the locket that contained her picture. She wanted him to know her, as her *boy*friend—nothing less. But when she turned back, Eli was still sitting there, waiting for her to say something else.

"You're welcome," she said slowly, forcing the words out of her mouth. She looked into Eli's dark eyes. "What are *friends* for?"

BEAUTY IS IN THE EYE OF THE BEHOLDER

The next morning, Lola stood in the living room in her Harry Potter pajamas, picking M&M's out of a Ming vase. She'd spent the entire night curled up in bed with Heath Bar, using his thick orange fur as a tissue. Her eyes were practically swollen shut and her face felt raw. Even worse, Stella had put her in charge of cleaning the living room. She'd just scraped pink frosting off the mantel, her teeth gritted the whole time. She shouldn't have been vacuuming ground chocolates from the rug, or scrubbing bloody icing from the floor. It was never her party in the first place.

She dropped the M&M's into a trash bag, shaking the sticky ones from her hands. She couldn't stop picturing Gunther's face, how he'd pulled away from her in disgust. *You aahh feeelthy! You smeeell like ze poo-poo!* She'd been so dim. She shouldn't have believed anyone—Ayana, Andie, or Gunther—when they said she could be a model. Because, somewhere deep down, she always knew the truth. Betsy Carmichael was right. She wasn't supposed to walk down the hall and have people look up to her; she wasn't supposed to be featured on the *Ashton News* as a person to watch. There were already enough girls like that at Ashton, and she already had her place. She was Lola "Days of the Week" Childs.

Stella appeared in the doorway in plaid boxers and a T-shirt. "Lola . . . I have a present for you." She was wearing bright yellow rubber gloves, a scrubbing brush in one hand and a bucket in the other. "Here. There are punch puddles all over the kitchen floor."

"Why can't *you* clean the floor?" Lola punted a cupcake in the middle of the Persian rug. Cate had already demanded she collect the plastic cups from the dining room, even though she hadn't set foot in there the entire night.

"I'm cleaning the foyer," Stella said as she brushed back her curls with the crook of her elbow. She'd been up since eight, pulling down the wall of Polaroids. She didn't have the energy to argue. Last night, their grandmum had come home early from her date. Margot had looked at the punch stain on the foyer wall and the cupcakes smashed into the floor and barely said a word. Apparently things with Walter Hodgeworth didn't go as well as she'd hoped. He preferred women in their fifties. *I look like I'm in my fifties!* she cried. She'd agreed the party could be "their secret" as long as the girls tidied the house first thing this morning, so that it was in perfect condition when Margot woke up. "Besides," Stella added, "Andie will help you."

Lola cringed at the sound of Andie's name. She should've realized Andie wasn't okay with her modeling. She was just waiting, looking for the perfect way to get back at her. Lola imagined her at Kyle's band practice, batting her eyelashes like a twit and tossing her hair over her shoulder the same way she'd showed Lola. She had probably decided to keep Kyle on call, in case Clay broke up with her. It just wasn't fair—to Lola, or to Kyle. Even if he hadn't been the best friend this week, Lola was sad just thinking about his face last night. He'd looked like he was about to cry. "Maybe I don't want Andie to help me," Lola mumbled.

"Please, Lola." Stella sighed. "Just do it for me." She dropped the bucket on the floor and disappeared into the foyer.

In the kitchen, Andie was kneeling on the ground, surrounded by a puddle of pink foam.

"Hey . . ." Andie said, trying hard to smile. Lola hadn't spoken to her since last night. She'd barricaded herself in her room, locking the bathroom door so Andie couldn't get in. Andie knew she was mad, but she just needed to explain. That one little lie about "Clay's sweatshirt" had snowballed, turning into something too big to control. "Can you pass the bucket?" she asked, breaking the silence.

Lola dumped some soapy water on the floor, splashing it right in Andie's face. Then she knelt down and started scrubbing, pretending she hadn't heard the question. "Lola, I can explain . . ." Andie started.

"Don't bother." Lola was scrubbing so hard she nearly took the finish off the wood. "I don't want to hear how you forgot to tell me you were going to Kyle's band practice. You just flirted with him because you were mad at me about Ayana. You're jealous I was modeling."

Andie swallowed hard. Just last week she'd flirted with Kyle to get back at Lola for the Ford go-see, but this time was different. Kyle was the one who'd showed up at the soccer game. Kyle was the one who'd IMed her. She hadn't set out to hurt Lola. The only thing she'd done wrong was like him back. "If I was so jealous, why would I help you do your makeup for the go-see? Why would I tell you to meet Gunther and help you pick out a dress to wear?" She looked Lola in the eyes. "I'm happy for you, I am. And I was going to tell you I'd been hanging out with Kyle eventually, but there was never a good time. You were upset about Pacific Sunwear, or Betsy Carmichael, or Gunther."

Lola stopped scrubbing, her fingers pink. It was true. Andie *had* helped her with modeling. But she still couldn't get past all the lies. The entire time she'd been texting Kyle, and IMing him, asking him to hang out, he'd been hanging out with Andie. Not once—but several times. She'd made her look like a fool. "Just tell me one thing—was that even Clay's sweatshirt in your room? Was I right? Was it Kyle's?"

Andie sat back on her heels. "Yeah. It was."

Lola winced. Kyle had given Andie a CD *and* his sweatshirt. He didn't just fancy her—he was bloody obsessed. Her mobile vibrated in her pocket and she darted into the living room, thankful to get away from her stepsister. She didn't want to think anymore about Kyle waiting for Andie outside Ashton after school, or asking her to play a one-on-one soccer match on the Great Lawn. She glanced at the ID, which said *Unavailable*. Abby's number in London was private, so they always used it when they prank-called Stella. Lola smiled for the first time all day. "Abby?"

"No, Lola. Hi. It's Ayana Bennington."

Lola imagined Ayana in her massive office, her four-inch heels crossed on top of her desk. Ayana was known for the thick black hair that fell past her butt, and Lola pictured it in a braid, wrapped around her neck like a scarf.

"I guess you heard about the shoot," Lola muttered.

"I did. Gunther just called." Lola's palms were so sweaty she was afraid the mobile would slip from her hands like a bar of soap. If she'd known it was Ayana, she never would've picked up.

"Ayana, it's just . . ." Lola began, her face feeling hot. She had hoped to be the model Ayana said she was. She had hoped she'd be able to walk into a room and look confident, assured, so everyone—including the girls at Ashton Prep—would like her. She'd hoped to keep her shoulders pulled back and her chin up, to show Gunther she was just like her mum—that she was *that* talented, *that* beautiful. But she knew now she'd never be Emma Childs. Sometimes Lola couldn't believe she was even her daughter.

She didn't need Ayana to tell her that.

"It's just nothing, my dear. Gunther developed the shots. He loves them."

"He does?" Lola squeezed the back of the couch, stunned. Heath Bar was working his claws into its arm, but she was so excited, she didn't want to ruin the moment by yelling at him.

"He wasn't thrilled about the shoot. But when he developed the shots they were beautiful. I told you—you have a very unique look." Lola bounced up and down on her heels. "You're the industry's new It girl. The billboard goes up in Times Square next week, and he wants to book you for the Light shoot. We'll discuss it all this week—just wanted to give you the good news."

"Yes, right," Lola said and hung up. She stared at her reflection in the gilded mirror on the wall. Her hair was still a little greasy, and she wasn't wearing her headband. But for the first time she noticed the bits of gold in her irises and the way her freckles spread evenly over her entire face. She realized she'd never had a single pimple, and her eyebrows arched in the center even though she'd never tweezed them the way most girls did. She pulled back her hair, revealing her ears. She'd always hated them. They still weren't her favorite feature, but right now they didn't seem so big, or so strange looking. Right now they were part of what made her "unique," and maybe even a little . . . pretty.

Lola smiled at her reflection. It didn't matter if Stella said she had Dumbo ears, or if her nose wasn't a perfect button like Cate's. It didn't matter if Kyle never looked at her the way he looked at Andie. Because for the first time she was looking at herself . . . and she liked what she saw.

She bounded into the foyer and up the stairs, not stopping until she reached her mum's room. She needed to share the news with someone. It had just happened, and already it felt like a good dream she never wanted to wake up from. Margot was still curled up in bed, watching a marathon of *As the World Turns* on SoapNet. "Have you luvs finished tidying up?" She asked. Her hair was flattened to her head and she was still in her silk pajamas. She was clutching a box of tissues in one hand.

"Grandmum . . ." Lola climbed onto the bed. She pressed her fingers into her freckled cheeks. "I'm going to be on Gunther's billboard."

Margot bolted upright. "That's brilliant!" she cried, and squeezed Lola to her chest. Lola inhaled the scent of Crème de la Mer face moisturizer. "Your mum is going to be so proud of you."

"Thanks," Lola said, waiting for Margot to say something else.

But she just took Lola's hand in her own and smiled. "Really, luv." Lola felt just the slightest pang of disappointment. She'd wanted her grandmum to jump up and down on the bed with her and demand they go get Pinkberry to celebrate. Or to be so bloody excited for her that she had to scream. She sometimes forgot that even if Margot wore halter dresses and heels, she was still a sixty-eight-year-old woman.

Her grandmum had done Lola's makeup for the Gutter shoot, but without one person, she never would've gotten the job. She would've still been upset about the Pacific Sunwear casting, or she would've written an e-mail to Ayana Bennington telling her to bugger off. Staring into her grandmum's green eyes, she realized she hadn't wanted to share the news with just anyone—she'd wanted to share it with *Andie.*

MAKING UP IS HARD TO DO

S tella stood outside a three-story town house on Seventieth Street, feeling like the eggs she had for breakfast might make a second appearance. She'd called Myra five times this morning, but she'd refused to pick up. Myra was Stella's first real friend in New York—the first one who wasn't related to her, at least. She was the only person Stella had told about her dad and Cloud McClean, and the only person Stella knew at school whom she hadn't met through Cate. She couldn't lose her over Blythe's bloody challenge.

Stella pressed down on the doorbell, her fingers trembling. After she'd finished cleaning the guest bathrooms (holding her nose the entire time), she'd gone shopping at the Manhattan Mall, a place she'd found through a Google search. She was now wearing a denim skirt, Myra's signature rainbow knee-highs, and a HOW'S MY DERIVING? tee. She'd even bought a sweater for Myra's ferret, Pythagoras, as an *I'm sorry* present (technically it was made for toy poodles, but she hoped it would do). It was a little extreme, but she needed to show Myra that she didn't care about what she wore—Stella cared about who she was. And she wanted to be friends with her, no matter what.

The front door swung open and Myra appeared, her blond hair pulled back into a tight bun. Her eyes were still a little swollen from the night before. Seeing Stella's outfit, she started to close the door. "Myra—wait!" Stella cried, catching it before it could shut. "Please?"

Myra crossed her arms over her chest. "What are you doing here?" She looked both ways down Seventieth Street, as though she were expecting to see Cate hiding behind her neighbor's garbage can. "Is this some sort of joke?"

"No," Stella said, pointing to her outfit. "These are my new socks and this my new T-shirt." She studied Myra's face, but her amber eyes revealed nothing. "I was planning on wearing them to school tomorrow. And the next day . . . until you forgive me."

Stella waited for Myra to smile, or laugh, but she didn't. Instead she tapped her foot, her clog keeping time like a metronome. "I can't forgive you if you don't apologize," she said finally.

"I was getting to that." Stella twisted one hand in the other, wringing it like a wet towel. She'd spent the entire walk to Myra's house rehearsing what she'd say, but now everything seemed inadequate. If Myra didn't want to be friends with her anymore, she couldn't argue, or convince herself Myra was overreacting. Because she knew that whatever happened—even if Myra threw a clog in her face—she deserved it. "I'm sorry, Myra, I am. And this is the only way I knew how to show you. I don't care about the stupid makeover, or if you wear your EASY AS π T-shirt every day for the rest of your life. Maybe things started with Blythe's challenge, but I'm lucky we became friends. You're smart, and funny, and . . . the best person I've met since I've been in New York."

Myra's face softened. "Do you really mean that?"

"More than anything. Here," Stella pulled the ferret-size present from her Marc Jacobs bag and pressed it into Myra's hands. "I bought this for Pythagoras."

Myra opened the box and held up the miniature argyle sweater. Stella had thought it was perfect for a ferret with a math-inspired nickname. For the first time since the incident yesterday, Myra smiled. "Thanks." She looked at Stella's outfit and let out a small laugh. "You're really going to wear that to school tomorrow?"

"I will if you want me to," Stella offered. She would've worn it for the entire year. Being popular seemed pointless now. She'd been popular in London, and all she had to show for it were two "best mates" who hadn't rung her once since she'd been in New York. Not to see how her mum's wedding was, or to hear about her first day at her new school. Not even to confirm that she hadn't gotten run over by a cab.

Myra shook her head. "That *would* be funny, but it's not necessary." She looked Stella in the eye, suddenly serious. "I can't be the third member of Chi Sigma, though. And I definitely can't be *Cate Sloane's* best friend. It's just not me." She straightened up, but her face still looked sad. "Besides, you spend every minute with her. I just don't see how this would work."

Stella let out a deep breath. Cate was her stepsister. It wasn't like she could avoid hanging out with her . . . even if she wanted to. But the reality was, right now they could hardly be considered friends. Cate had only said two words to her all morning: *Plastic bag?* she'd asked, tossing Stella one. Stella knew Cate was mad she'd abandoned the party, but she'd been upset about Myra. The last thing she'd wanted to do after their fight was field questions from *Ashton News.*

Stella and Cate both couldn't stand the headmistress's high-pitched voice. They both laughed at the way Winston hummed Sinatra whenever he thought he was in a room alone. And they both loved an afternoon of shopping on Madison Avenue, trying on dresses that would only be appropriate for an art auction at Sotheby's.

But lately it felt like they were too different. Yes, Cate had liked Myra. But it was only because she was a way to prove to Blythe that they were just as much of a sorority as Beta Sigma Phi. Stella liked Myra for who she was—the person who thought Cloud McClean was a blue-haired eleventh-grader. Stella tugged on a blond curl, her decision made. "I don't need to spend every minute with Cate," she said. "I just need you—to be my friend."

Myra stepped out of the doorway and put her tiny arms around Stella. It wasn't her usual, rib cage–breaking hug, but it was enough to squeeze tears into Stella's eyes. "I still am," she said quietly.

SUPERMODELS HAVE MORE IMPORTANT THINGS TO WORRY ABOUT

"And you say," Kyle's voice sang, "It's o-kay, and that's o-kay with meeee." Andie hit stop on her Bose stereo and retreated to the bed, pulling her red quilt around her. She'd listened to Kyle's CD straight through, each song making her feel a little worse. He wouldn't pick up her phone calls or respond to her texts, and when she signed onto Facebook she discovered he'd deleted her from his friend list. He wasn't just mad—he was trying to surgically remove her from his life.

She sat back on the bed, a lump rising in the back of her throat. It was useless. He'd seen her kissing Clay Calhoun. She couldn't truly explain the situation to him, even if he gave her the chance. She'd have to tell him about Lola, and how she'd always liked him, and how Andie had created a whole lie to protect her . . . or to at least try to. As awful a sister as she'd been the past week, Lola's secrets weren't hers to tell.

There was a knock on the door, and Lola peered in. Her hair

was still stringy, and the knees of her pajama pants were crusted with pink frosting. "Can I come in?"

Andie nodded, smoothing back her bangs. She knew how it all must've looked to Lola: bad. Very, very bad. The truth was, Andie *did* feel jealous whenever Lola mentioned Gunther by his first name, and some small part of her *didn't* want Lola to be modeling in *Vogue*. But that wasn't why she liked Kyle. She liked the way he glanced up at her while he was singing, as if every song were written just for her. She liked that he always sent her links to *Saturday Night Live* clips, or silly YouTube videos, or anything he thought would make her laugh. And she liked how he had printed the CD cover on his computer and carefully handwritten the names of all the new songs. She just liked *him*. It was simple.

"Lola," she started, searching for the right words, "Kyle showed up at my soccer scrimmage and we started talking, but I didn't know how to tell you. So I just made up that stupid lie about dating Clay."

Lola sat down on the edge of the bed, looking at Andie like she'd just said something in Chinese. "But you told every person at the party you were a couple. You were holding hands. You're *not* dating him?"

Andie rubbed her eyes, which were still pink from crying. "No. I didn't know what to say when you asked me about the sweatshirt, so I lied. And then I had to cover it up by pretending he was my boyfriend. When everyone was cheering for us to kiss, I didn't want to, but I didn't know what else to do."

Andie pulled the comforter tighter around her, so only her

head poked out. She'd never been good at lying. She'd known that ever since third grade, when her dad caught her stealing his silk handkerchiefs to use as Barbie blankets. Still, for a moment it had looked like everything would work out—Clay would leave the party, Kyle would arrive, and Andie wouldn't have to tell Lola about any of it until it was the right time. But maybe that was the problem. There never was a "right time." Even now. "I was just afraid to tell you," she started. "I like Kyle."

Lola wished Andie hadn't offered that information. It hurt enough to think about how Kyle fancied Andie. She didn't want to think about how they both fancied each other. Lola imagined them walking around the reservoir together, holding hands, or Kyle coming over every weekend to see *Andie*, to pick *her* up to go to the movies or play foosball in their den. Lola would never want to leave her room again. "I didn't come here to talk about Kyle," she said, changing the subject. "I wanted to tell you my good news. Gunther liked the shots. He's going to use them after all."

Andie threw her arms around Lola, letting the blanket fall from her shoulders. "I told you!" she screamed. Andie bounced up and down on the bed, excited. This was going to change everything for Lola—in a good way. Since she'd arrived in New York she'd kept asking Andie how she could be different, prettier, cooler. She wanted to be someone Kyle would like and Betsy Carmichael wouldn't make fun of. Maybe now she would finally relax, and just be herself. Andie liked the real Lola—with her spastic hand-clapping and fur-covered Gap hoodies—best of all. "When does the billboard go up?"

"Next week," Lola managed. Andie was hugging her so tight she could barely talk.

"Your face is going to be in Times Square? I can't wait for everyone at Ashton to see it." Andie threw herself across the bed dramatically, as if Lola had just told her *she'd* be modeling for Gunther Gunta. "My stepsister is a supermodel," she said, to no one in particular.

"I can't wait for them to see it either." Lola smoothed down her blond hair and smiled. *That* was the reaction she'd wanted. She needed someone who knew what life at Ashton Prep was like before, and who could understand what it would be like after. Betsy Carmichael would regret ever saying anything about her knickers.

Her gaze settled on the collage above Andie's bed. The Chloé ad with Andie's smiling face pasted on the body of a model was still there, in plain sight. Modeling had always been Andie's dream. She DVR'd *America's Next Top Model* every week, and watched it (at the very least) three times, pausing on different poses and trying to imitate them. Lola didn't have a bloody clue who Gunther Gunta was—Andie had had to tell her.

She thought about Kyle's face at the party, when he saw Andie snogging Clay. Then she glanced at Andie's eyes, which were red. Her stomach sank with guilt. Lola didn't love the idea of them being together, but she also didn't want to be the thing keeping them apart. "So you really fancy Kyle?" she asked.

Andie examined Lola's face, nervous that she was still mad or upset. But her green eyes were wide, and her nose wasn't twitching—not even a little. "Yeah, I do. I really do," Andie said.

"It doesn't matter, though. He won't even talk to me. I called him and e-mailed, but nothing." Andie twisted the bottom of her T-shirt so hard she thought it might rip. She tried to imagine things if they were the other way around—if *Lola* had been sneaking around with *her* crush. The worst part was, no matter how hard she tried, she couldn't. Because the truth was, Lola would never do that to her. "I'm sorry that I lied to you. I was just scared that you'd hate me."

Lola sat down next to Andie and shook her shoulders a bit. "I don't hate you." It was the truth. She'd been upset about Kyle, but she hadn't seen him in almost a week. Whenever they did talk, he kept on about what good mates they were. Sure, they'd been best friends as children, but she was starting to feel like she didn't even know him anymore. His Facebook page had a hundred pictures of him onstage with his band, his sweaty hair held back by some girly-looking headband. There were shots of him playing soccer at Donalty, and he even had a fan page for his band. Lola liked to ride horses, was first-chair viola, and had never been to a concert (unless you counted the Philharmonic at Royal Albert Hall). They weren't exactly two sides of the same coin. Maybe Kyle was supposed to be with someone different, someone who was actually interested in the same things he was. Someone like . . . Andie. "I'm just glad Clay's not your boyfriend. He's a real arse. He kept on for five whole minutes about how he threw a tuna fish sandwich at some bloke's head." She laughed, feeling her anger sliding away. Besides, as of today she was a model—*Gunther Gunta's* model. It was hard to be mad about anything right now.

"At least you didn't have to hear about how Brandon peed in a Pepsi bottle on their camping trip," Andie mumbled.

Lola let out a laugh, but Andie's face was still sad. Kyle's sweatshirt was slung over Andie's desk chair and Lola stared at it, an idea forming. Even if Kyle wouldn't talk to Andie, he would talk to her. . . .

LOLABEAN: SAW YOU RUN OUT ON SATURDAY

STRIKER15: I KINDA HAD TO

LOLABEAN: ANDIE TOLD ME THAT YOU GUYS WERE
HANGING OUT

STRIKER15: WE'RE NOT ANYMORE

LOLABEAN: IF IT'S BECAUSE OF CLAY . . . IT'S NOT WHAT IT
LOOKED LIKE

STRIKER15: ??

LOLABEAN: SHE DOESN'T FANCY HIM—SHE FANCIES YOU

STRIKER15: THEN WHY DID SHE MAKE OUT WITH HIM?

LOLABEAN: HE JUST SNOGGED HER. SHE DIDN'T EVEN
WANT HIM TO

STRIKER15: WHAT? REALLY?

LOLABEAN: EVERYONE WAS YELLING AT CLAY TO DO IT

LOLABEAN: ANDIE WAS GOING TO STOP HIM BUT HE DID
IT ANYWAY

STRIKER15: YEAH?

LOLABEAN: COME OVER TONIGHT

LOLABEAN: U SHOULD TALK TO HER

STRIKER15: I DON'T KNOW

LOLABEAN: PLEASE?

STRIKER15: OK . . . I'LL SEE YOU AT 7

LOLABEAN: GOOD

STRIKER15: ANOTHER THING—R WE COOL?

STRIKER15: I WAS WORRIED THAT MAYBE U'D BE UPSET
ABOUT ME HANGING OUT WITH ANDIE

STRIKER 15: THAT'S WHY I DIDN'T TELL YOU I WAS COMING
TO THE PARTY

LOLABEAN: NO—WE'RE ACE
STRIKER15: PROMISE?
LOLABEAN: ABSO-BLOODY-LUTELY
STRIKER15: THANKS
STRIKER15: UR THE BEST, STICKS

IT'S CALLED A "SECRET" PASSAGE FOR A REASON

Later that night, Cate shuffled through the "Green Club" folder, searching for clues. All day, Eli's words had kept running through her head, like a bad song that was stuck on repeat. *Does she have a boyfriend? She just seems cool.* He hadn't said Stella was pretty, put together, or had cool hair (which Cate hated to admit, but she did)—things anyone could tell by passing her in the street. They had hung out before—but *when*? She studied a photo of Eli and Braden Pennyworth playing Ultimate Frisbee in the North Meadow, and one of Eli standing alone on the corner of Eighty-fourth and Amsterdam. There was only one person in the background. Unless Stella had disguised herself as a homeless man in a pilot's helmet, it wasn't her.

Just then Cate's iPhone buzzed.

DANNY: I LOOKED INTO YR QUERY RE: STELLA. NO NEW INTELLIGENCE 2 REPORT

Cate threw the phone down on her bed, annoyed. If she had to hire Danny to follow Stella around for a week, she would. She needed to know the truth. She hoped it was all an innocent mistake, that Stella had bumped into Eli on his stoop and simply forgotten to mention it to her. But after the incident in the garden, Eli had wandered around the party like a lost child, hoping Stella might come downstairs. Then he'd asked Cate (twice!) to let Stella know he'd been there. The more she thought about it, the less innocent it seemed.

Cate had been in the town house the entire day, and she was starting to feel a little stir crazy—or maybe just crazy. She needed to take a walk to clear her head. She took off downstairs, stopping in the den to grab the last of the trash bags.

She pushed out the front door and hurled the plastic bags on the sidewalk, slightly satisfied by the *thwack!* sound they made. The last evidence of the party was gone. But cleaning up the town house was the easy part. Doing damage control tomorrow at school would be harder. She'd have to field more questions about Myra's failed makeover, and more girls asking her about "the hot Haverford guy" she was talking to. Just yesterday she'd imagined saying "that's my boyfriend," but now that was clearly out of the question.

Just then the front door of Eli Punch's town house swung open. A woman in her forties jogged down the steps and a muscular man with a thick brown beard followed close behind her. "Easy, Holden," Eli called, as a yellow Labrador retriever dragged him outside. Eli pulled the dog back, his legs whipped by its tail.

Cate smoothed back her hair, suddenly nervous. Eli's entire

family looked like they'd stepped out of *Runner's World* magazine. Eli's dad wore a Nike tank top and sleek black running sneakers, his mom's jet-black hair was in a tight ponytail, and Eli was wearing his blue Haverford warm-up pants. "Hi," Cate said, pulling her bathrobe tighter around her body.

"This must be your new neighbor friend." The man combed his beard with his hand.

Cate cringed. There was that word again—*friend.* Even if Cate wasn't in a place to turn down friends (her grand total was currently one, *if* she counted Stella), she would never be friends with Eli. She would never sit next to him without wanting to hold his hand. She would never listen to him talk about Stella without feeling like he was squeezing her heart with a wrench.

"Yeah, this is Cate." Eli smiled. "You guys go. I'll catch up." His parents ran off toward Central Park, the yellow Lab in tow.

"Hey, Eli," Cate started, scraping her slippers against the sidewalk. "I'm glad we ran into each other. There's something I meant to ask you." Cate searched Eli's dark eyes. "How do you know Stella?"

Eli raised an eyebrow. "She didn't tell you? She found a door in her closet. It goes between our two houses. She busted a hole right through my bedroom wall." He let out a little laugh.

Cate dug her fingernails into her palm. "A door?" she squeaked.

"Yeah. That's how we met." He glanced toward the park. "Sorry, I have to go," he said. Then he took off down Eighty-second Street. "See you later."

"Right. . . ." Cate mumbled, but Eli was already turning the corner. She'd lived in her town house her entire life. When she was little her mother had used Stella's new room as a library, reading her *Green Eggs and Ham* and *Goodnight Moon* in the daybed up there. Just this summer, Cate had kept her entire winter wardrobe in that closet, finally moving it to some musty storage space once Stella arrived. But she'd never noticed a door—ever. It was too ridiculous to believe, like a magical beanstalk or a poison apple. It was something out of a fairy tale.

Cate ran into the house and up one flight of stairs, then the next, and the next, not stopping until she reached Stella's room. She entered the closet, her heart beating fast, as though she were on a treasure hunt and she'd finally found the treasure. The walk-in was packed with clothes, and she had to kick stray blouses out of her way just to get through. There were baskets of Prada belts and Fendi scarves, and a whole wall of designer shoes. She spun around, pushing aside a rack of casual dresses to try and find the door. She moved a rack of J Brand jeans, and a stack of folded sweaters on a shelf. Then she noticed a long sliver of light on her leg. Sure enough, on the back wall, right between two green Diane von Furstenberg blouses, she could see the edge of something that looked like a passageway. She pushed back some tops and found the door, the mint green paint chipped around its frame.

Cate sat down, her back pressing into Stella's shoe collection. Eli was right. This whole time, while Cate was going to his basketball games and planning their first kiss, Stella was sneaking in and out of his room via secret passage. No wonder he liked her so much. She probably talked to him about *Catcher in the Rye,* or how she'd heard the beaches in Westport were calmer than the ones in the Hamptons, just because they were on the Long Island Sound. She probably used every single piece of intel *Cate* had collected to convince Eli *she* loved yellow Labs, that *she* played girls' basketball in London, that *she* would be a perfect girlfriend.

Cate felt the tears welling in her eyes. Forget Chi Sigma—nothing had changed. Stella was still lying to her face, still scheming behind her back. Maybe she hadn't been able to win Blythe, Priya, and Sophie away from her, but now she'd gone after Eli. Cate turned her diamond earring between her fingers. It was times like these she missed her mom the most. Everything was different now. Winston had Emma, Andie had Lola, Stella had Eli, and Cate had no one.

Blythe's words repeated on loop in Cate's ears. *It's for the best,* she'd said. *Come back to us.* Cate stared at the door. She'd spent so much time worrying about Blythe, making up those lies about her kicking puppies in the head and planning that silly party so Chi Sigma could be more popular than Beta Sigma Phi. It seemed a little . . . *wrong* now. She and Blythe had always been better as a team. They'd stayed close through Blythe's parents' divorce, through Cate losing her mom, through Blythe spending every summer traveling with her dad. Their friendship had never been a problem—until Stella moved to New York.

Cate reached into the pocket of her jeans and pulled out her iPhone, her hands trembling as she dialed the number. *Pick up,* she thought, listening to it ring. *Please pick up.*

"Hello?" Blythe asked. She sounded formal, like the receptionist at Winston's bank.

"Blythe?" Cate choked out, the tears streaming down her face. She twisted the string of her pajama pants around her hand, so tight her fingers turned pink. There was silence on the end of the line. "I need to talk to you."

"Are you crying?" Blythe asked, her voice softening. Cate tried to say yes, but she just mumbled, the tears wetting the phone.

"I'm sorry about Eli—about everything." Cate wiped her cheek with back of her hands. "I want to be friends again."

"Cate, I told you you could come back," Blythe continued. Her voice was steady, calm, reassuring. Like maybe she'd had her cell phone in her lap all day, just waiting for the call. "This whole thing has gotten completely out of control."

Cate let out a deep breath. "I know. I miss you."

"I miss you too," Blythe said. Cate could practically hear her nodding over the phone.

"Then why did you do it?" Cate squeezed the phone tightly. Maybe Blythe really hadn't meant to tell Myra about the challenge. Maybe they'd both gotten carried away with the competition for Eli. But there was one thing Cate couldn't understand. Blythe knew how much Chi Beta Phi meant to her, and yet she'd stolen the presidency out from under her. "Why did you turn Sophie and Priya against me?"

"I wasn't trying to turn them against you!" Blythe cried. "You said it yourself—I was 'in your shadow.' I just wanted to show you I could do something on my own. Without you. How was I supposed to know you'd start a new sorority with Stella and *Myra Granberry*?"

Cate smiled despite herself. Her supposed friendship with

Myra wasn't something *anyone* could have predicted. Still, she'd always thought Blythe was fine being her second in command—when they danced at the annual talent show she always insisted Cate be in the front, because she was uncomfortable on stage. She nominated Cate every year for class president, and she was the one who'd suggested Cate lead Chi Beta Phi in the first place. "You should've said something if you were unhappy."

"Maybe I should have." There was a long pause. Cate could only hear Blythe's breath on the other end of the line. "Look," she said finally, "I'm tired of fighting with you. It just seems . . . wrong."

Cate dug her toes into the Juicy blouse on Stella's floor. "I know. I hate it too." Even if she burned every memento she and Blythe had ever made, she couldn't erase the last nine years of their friendship. Blythe came over every Mother's Day and brought her a present, just so she wouldn't feel so alone. And it was Blythe who called her from her vacation in South Africa last year, when Sophie and Priya had forgotten her birthday. She'd never find a friend as good as her . . . and definitely not in Stella. She glanced at the door, feeling a little queasy. "And you're not going to believe this. . . ." Cate lowered her voice to a whisper. "Eli Punch likes Stella."

"Stella?" Blythe said. "How does he even know her?"

Cate moved the dresses back in front of the passageway and sighed. Out of sight—out of mind. At least for now. "It's a long story. Are you home?"

"Yeah—come over."

Cate hung up the phone, feeling more like herself than she

had all week. There were only a few things she could rely on: the sun rising every morning, Barneys' annual warehouse sale, and the Chi Beta Phis. Without them, she felt like someone had surgically removed her heart. She ran down the stairs and out the front door, not bothering to look back.

EPILOGUE

Everybody needs a friend. Some, like Andie and Lola, find kinship in sisters.

Others, like Stella, find the most satisfying friendship in the most unexpected of places. Even if it involves wearing rainbow-colored socks.

And still others, like Cate, find comfort in those who've been there all along (a selective memory helps, of course).

All's well that ends well, or so they say. But having a friend doesn't mean you automatically forget your enemies . . . especially when they live under the same roof. For now, the cozy brick town house on Eighty-second Street is quiet.

But everything can change in a New York minute.

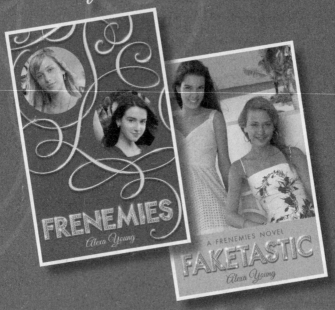